The third wav...
Kai made no...
the last second, he spun his board around and paddled hard, just managing to catch the wave. A second later the black guy dropped in on him. Kai had expected that, and as the guy dropped down the face of the wave, Kai put his weight on the toeside rail, forcing his board up and over the other surfer.

The black guy did a nice sweeping bottom turn and headed back up the face. Kai squatted and drove the nose of the long board down, picking up speed and outrunning the short boarder, who hit the lip and wheeled around. Once again Kai forced the long board up into the wave and then down, but it was no longer a contest. The wave was losing its energy and there was no way the black guy could possibly catch him.

Kai dropped down on his board, turned it around, and began to paddle over the fourth wave of the set.

And that was when the big guy hit him.

**Look for the next books in the
Impact Zone series:**

Cut Back
Close Out

Coming soon from Simon Pulse

**And get hooked on some of Todd Strasser's
other Simon & Schuster books . . .**

Can't Get There from Here
Give a Boy a Gun
How I Created My Perfect Prom Date
Here Comes Heavenly
Buzzard's Feast: Against the Odds

IMPACT ZONE
TAKE OFF

TODD STRASSER

Simon Pulse
New York   London   Toronto   Sydney

First Simon Pulse edition May 2004

Text copyright © 2004 by Todd Strasser

SIMON PULSE
An imprint of Simon & Schuster
Children's Publishing Division
1230 Avenue of the Americas
New York, NY 10020

Designed by Ann Sullivan
The text of this book was set in Bembo.

Printed in the United States of America
10 9 8 7 6 5 4 3 2 1

Library of Congress Control Number 2003114110

ISBN 0-689-87029-9

In memory of Jill Tuck, as fine a mother, surfer's wife, and all-around wonderful person as most of us will ever have the privilege to know

This book is dedicated to Fran Lantz, mother, writer, surfer, brave and spirited human being.

One

Another 3 A.M. escape.

"Come on, back the damn thing up," Pat Herter said in the dark somewhere behind the box truck. Sitting in the passenger seat of the truck, Kai Herter squinted into the side-view mirror. He could hardly see his father in the deep shadows of the night. In the driver's seat Kai's half brother, Sean, peered into his side-view mirror as he slowly backed the truck down the narrow, unlit alley.

"Come on, we don't have all night," Pat grumbled like an invisible specter behind them. "Move it."

"You try backing this thing up without lights," Sean said through the open window.

"With my eyes closed, junior," Pat answered. He took off his thick, square glasses and polished them with the tail of his red-plaid shirt.

In the truck's cab Sean turned to Kai and smirked. "Hear that? With his eyes closed. Big turd can't see squat with his eyes open. What's he gonna see with 'em closed?"

Screak! A loud metallic scrape ripped through the silence and the truck jolted to a stop.

"You hit the damn wall, you retard!" Pat snapped.

"I wouldn't've if you'd let me put the headlights on," Sean shot back through the truck window.

"Oh, sure, put the damn headlights on," Pat said. "And while you're at it, call the landlord and tell him we're takin' off. Hell, forget the landlord, just call the damn cops."

"Screw you." Sean put the truck into forward and eased away from the wall, then straightened it out and started to back through the dark again. In the passenger seat Kai yawned. It was hard to believe that his life had come to this: stuck with these two bozos, scrambling from town to town, and scam to scam, always a half step ahead of the law and a battalion of bill collectors.

"Okay, that's good," Pat said behind them.

Sean yanked on the parking brake and cut the engine. Kai pushed open the door and jumped down to the ground. The night air was steamy and still. The alley, quiet. The odor of rotting garbage hung in the air, thanks to the Dumpster behind the Chinese take-out place next door. In the faint light cast by a distant streetlamp, Kai watched Pat prop open the back door to the T-shirt shop with a brick.

"Okay, let's go!" Pat whispered like it was some kind of stealth military operation and not just a couple of con artists skipping out on three months' rent.

Kai went through the door and into the dark T-shirt shop. The chemical smell of cheap polyester-and-cotton T-shirts and the ink of heat transfers invaded his nose. Near him Pat shined a small flashlight on a dozen oven-size cardboard boxes filled with T-shirts. "These first."

Kai grabbed one of the boxes by the edge and dragged it to the door. Outside, Sean waited to help lift the heavy boxes into the back of the truck. Each box was packed with a couple of hundred T-shirts or dozens of sweatshirts. The worst were the children's sizes, which could have up to a thousand in a box. Together, Sean and Kai heaved each box into the back of the truck. Sweat began to drip down Kai's forehead. He wiped it away with the sleeve of his T-shirt and went into the shop, while Sean jumped in the truck and pushed the box all the way in.

"Come on, hurry up," Pat muttered impatiently inside the shop. He was dumping piles of colorful vinyl stickers and heat transfers into a big black plastic garbage bag.

Kai grabbed the next box and started to drag it toward the door. He was fifteen years old with black hair and blue-green eyes. In the past year he'd probably grown five inches. His shoulders had broadened and his waist had thinned and if he went a day without shaving it showed. He didn't care much about these physical changes, except that it meant that he was getting older and stronger and closer to the day when he would ditch these clowns and have a life of his own.

He dragged the next box through the door and out to the back of the truck, where Sean was waiting. His half brother was twenty-one or twenty-two, short and thin with unruly brown hair, a bad case of acne, and small yellow teeth. He wasn't really a bad guy. Just a stooge and a follower and Pat's hand puppet. Sean didn't seem to have the brains to realize that he didn't have to let Pat push him around.

Together, Sean and Kai started to lift the box. There was a loud ripping sound followed by a thump, and the box suddenly felt a lot lighter.

A heap of white T-shirts lay on the ground at their feet.

"Crap," Sean muttered. "What do we do now?"

"Go into the shop and get some tape," Kai said. Things that seemed incredibly obvious to him weren't always obvious to Sean.

Sean went into the store and came back with the tape. He was followed, of course, by Pat. Kai's father was a short, pudgy man with dark, unkempt hair and those thick, square glasses that made him look like the Alien Frog Beast from planet Dimwit. "What happened here?"

Kai was tempted to ask him what the hell he thought had happened, since it was clear that the bottom of the box had torn open. But with Pat things couldn't just happen for no reason. There always had to be someone to blame.

"You should have checked the bottom before you picked it up," the Alien Frog Beast said while Kai took the tape from Sean and started to retape the box.

Kai didn't bother to answer. He quickly fixed the box, and he and Sean started to throw the T-shirts back in. Meanwhile Pat went back into the store and dragged out the garbage bag filled with heat transfers, the colorful designs people wanted on their T-shirts. He threw the bag into the truck. Kai and Sean were still dumping the spilled shirts back into the box.

"Come on, come on, we don't have all day," Pat grumbled.

"It's night," Sean said.

Pat stared at him through those thick glasses. "It is?"

"Yeah, sure," Sean started to say, then caught himself. "Wait a minute. You know it's night."

Pat shook his head wearily. "I got a genius for a son." He went back into the shop.

"Someday I'm gonna—," Sean muttered, once his father was out of earshot.

The alley lit up. Sean froze. Squinting in

the sudden bright light, Kai peeked around the side of the truck. Headlights were coming toward them. For a split second Kai hoped they might be from a garbage truck coming to empty the restaurant's Dumpster, but the engine didn't have the deep rumble of a truck's. It was a car.

"What do we do?" Sean's high-pitched whisper was etched with panic.

"Let's see who it is," Kai whispered back.

The car stopped twenty feet from the truck, its headlights blinding in the dark. Kai and Sean shielded their eyes with their hands. Maybe it was someone who got lost and made a wrong turn down the alley. Kai tried to peer through the lights. A door opened. He saw the silhouette of a figure step out. Suddenly another beam flashed on and swept around the truck and alley.

It had to be a cop.

Two

"**W**hat's goin' on here?" the cop asked in a deep southern, good-ole-boy accent. But there was nothing friendly about the tone. He shined the flashlight beam back and forth between Kai and Sean.

"Nothing," Kai said.

"Looks like somethin's goin' on. What y'all doin'?"

"Uh . . ." Kai had to think fast. "We're unloading."

"No, we're not," Sean said.

Kai shot him a look telling him to keep his mouth shut, but it was too late. The cop's free hand moved toward the holstered gun on his belt. He flashed the light into Kai's face.

"Well, which is it, son?" he asked, his tone growing even edgier. "Loadin' or unloadin'?"

"Unloading," Kai said.

The flashlight beam shifted to Sean. "And what do you'all say, son?"

"Uh, unloading," Sean answered.

"Well, good, I'm glad we got that settled," the cop said, keeping the light on Sean. "Now let's see if you boys can agree on just what you're unloadin'."

"T-shirts for the shop," Kai said.

The flashlight jumped back to Kai. "I didn't ask you, son. I asked your friend."

"He's right," Sean stammered.

"Y'all know it's three o'clock in the morning?" said the cop. "Kind of strange hour to be unloadin' T-shirts, ain't it?"

"Well, uh, we got in late and this truck's borrowed from a friend," Kai said. "We have to get it back to him by morning."

A metallic clank came from inside the store. The flashlight beam jumped from the boys' faces to the door behind them. "Somebody else back there?"

"Just our dad," Kai said, wondering if that would make it seem even less likely that they'd be involved in something illegal. After all, what kind of father would want to include his own sons in criminal activities?

"Y'all tell him to get out here right now," said the cop.

"Yes, sir." Kai turned toward the door, considering the possibilities. He could try to help save their butts, or he could just fess up and face the consequences—probably jail time for Pat, who already had a criminal record. Possibly some kind of suspended sentence for Sean. And for himself, no doubt a foster home here in the landlocked heart of the Deep South. Forget that. As eager as he was to get out of this crappy grifter's life, that wouldn't do at all. He'd be better off sticking with the two-jerk circus until it landed someplace where he wanted to put down roots. Then he'd cut free, get a job, and save up until he had enough money to go back home.

Kai stepped through the doorway into the dark shop. Pat was standing in a shadow just inside the door. It was obvious that he'd been listening.

"What's he want?" Kai's father whispered.

"To know whether we're unloading or loading," Kai whispered back. "I told him we were unloading 'cause then we can't be stealing, right? And I told him we're doing it in the middle of the night because we have to get the truck back to our friend in the morning."

Pat smiled. "Hey, that's good. You'd make a good crook."

Don't hold your breath, Pop, Kai thought.

"Hey, y'all in there, come on back out here now," the cop called from out in the alley.

"You might want to bring a copy of the store lease to prove you really do business here," Kai suggested, then went back out. Once again it took a moment for his eyes to adjust to the glare of the bright lights aimed at him.

"I thought y'all said you were getting your father," said the cop.

"He went to get the papers to show that he really owns the place," Kai explained.

"Just tell him to get on out here so's I can get a good look at him," the cop said.

"Hey, Dad," Kai said loudly. He'd never called Pat "dad" before and he didn't like the way it felt. "The police officer wants you to come out here right now."

Pat popped out of the back of the shop. With one hand he shielded his eyes. In the other he carried a manila envelope. "What's the problem?" he asked as if it wasn't obvious.

"Y'all the owner of this here shop?" the cop asked.

"Yes, officer, is something wrong?" Pat said.

"First I'd like to see some identification," said the cop. "Y'all come on over here nice and slow and put whatever y'all got on the hood of this vehicle."

Pat did as he was told, going around the truck and putting his wallet and the envelope within the cop's reach and then backing away. They waited while the cop went through the wallet and found the driver's license and matched it to the name on the lease.

"Derek Cartman?" the cop said.

"That's right, sir," Pat answered.

"Could y'all tell me how come the name on your driver's license says Cartman, but this truck here's registered to a Dan Marsh?"

"Uh . . ." Pat's mouth fell open.

"Like I said before," Kai cut in. "It's our friend's truck."

The flashlight snagged him again. "Now, you listen up, son. When I want an answer from you, I'll let y'all know. Otherwise y'all keep your mouth shut, understand?" The flashlight beam swung back to Pat. "Right now I'd like an answer from you, mister."

"It's our friend's van," Pat answered simply.

The cop was quiet for a moment. Kai held his breath. He knew they were a hair away from getting busted. And that meant he was a second away from becoming Kai Herter, ward of the state and new candidate for the foster-care system. The cop shined his light at Kai and Sean. "How about you two? Got any ID?"

Just as Pat had done, Kai and Sean put their wallets on the cruiser's hood and backed away. The cop picked up Kai's wallet first and aimed his light into it.

"Kay?"

"It's Kai," Kai said. "Rhymes with sky."

The cop nodded and looked in Sean's wallet. Then he closed it and put it back on the patrol car's hood. He shined his flashlight at Pat. "Sir, would y'all explain to me how come your last name's Cartman and their last names are Herter?"

"He's our stepdad," Kai said.

The beam glared straight into his eyes. "Son of a gun," the cop growled. "Y'all don't listen too good, do ya?"

"Sorry, officer," Kai said.

The cop went quiet again. Kai wondered what he was thinking. Whatever it was, he seemed to make up his mind. He motioned toward the back door to the patrol car. "Y'all get in here right now."

Kai felt the air leave his lungs. This was it. They were going down.

Three

"Is something wrong, officer?" Pat asked again, as if, being some kind of model citizen, he couldn't imagine what the problem might be.

"Can't say just yet," the cop answered, holding the patrol car door open for them. "Y'all just get in and we'll see."

Kai, Sean, and Pat slid into the back of the patrol car. The rear seat was caged on all sides, and the door handles and window cranks had been removed. The three of them sat shoulder to shoulder.

"Y'all know how this works, don'tcha boys," the cop said. "Y'all be locked in the back here while I go have me a look around.

Now while I'm gone, don't y'all do anything you're gonna regret, okay?"

The door slammed shut. In the headlights they watched the cop walk down the alley toward the truck.

"What's gonna happen?" Sean whimpered.

"You heard him," Pat grumbled, then mimicked the officer's accent. "He's gonna have him a look around."

"We're not going to jail, are we?" Sean's voice got high when he was scared.

"Just shut up," Pat said.

"I—I'm—," Sean whined.

"I said shut up," Pat growled.

Kai sat quietly. He tried to think of what was in the store or in the truck that the cop might find suspicious. He wondered what kind of foster family he'd wind up with, and if he'd ever see Hawaii again.

They listened to the hum of the patrol car's engine and the occasional burst of static from the radio. The air in the car was moist and still. Kai had been in a cop car only once before. It brought back bad memories.

In the headlights they watched the cop return from the shop. Under one arm he was carrying two hooded sweatshirts, one pink and the other gray. He came back to the patrol car and opened the door. "Okay, y'all can get on out."

They did as they were told. The cop handed them their wallets. "Well, Mr. Cartman, looks like everything's in order. Just a kind of strange time to be unloading a truck around here, if you ask me. Y'all understand that I had to check it out?"

"I understand completely, officer," Pat said. "You have a job to do and store owners like myself appreciate it. For all you know we could have been a bunch of thieves cleaning the place out."

The cop seemed to pause for a moment, as if wondering if there was something mocking in Pat's tone.

"I see you found some items you liked," Pat quickly added.

The cop looked down at the sweatshirts. "My wife and daughter, they just love stuff like this."

"Then please, accept them as a token of my appreciation for the fine job you officers do," Pat said.

"Y'all sure about that?" asked the cop.

"Absolutely."

"Well, thank you, sir. That's mighty kind of you. You boys take her easy, all right?" He got into the patrol car, put the sweatshirts on the passenger seat, and started to back down the alley.

As the cop car turned and disappeared into the dark, Kai felt a hand slap him on the back. Pat was beaming like a proud father. It was the kind of look fathers gave sons who'd just hit a home run or gotten an A on a test. Only Kai got it for BSing a cop. How bent was that?

The proud look on Pat's face didn't last. "Okay, back to work. We've still got a lot of stuff to move before the sun comes up. Sean, you get the hot press. Kai, there's more boxes that need to go in the truck. We're gettin' the hell out of here before the next cop shows up."

They packed everything they could into the truck. Phones, fax, computer, display racks and cases, mirrors, shelving, the tiny "security" cameras Pat aimed into the changing rooms so he could sit in the back office all day and watch women try on T-shirts. By 5 A.M. the sky was starting to lighten. Gray clouds to the east were beginning to turn pink. They jumped in the truck and headed out of town.

Kai knew it wasn't only the cops Pat was worried about. It was the landlord who was owed several months of back rent. Pat also owed money to the phone and utility companies, the T-shirt suppliers, and the company that made the heat transfers.

They were on the highway heading north. Sean driving. Kai in the middle of the bench seat. Pat on the passenger side, studying a map while a smoldering cigarette dangled from the corner of his mouth. Claiming he was legally blind so that he could qualify for veterans' benefits, Pat rarely drove even though he could read a road map in the dim dusky light. His eyes were good enough so that he always passed the vision test for every new driver's license. A new license for each new state, but always with a fake name based on a character from *South Park*—Pat and Sean's favorite TV show. It often seemed to Kai that his father scammed everyone he could, less for the money than for the sheer enjoyment of getting away with it.

In the rattling truck cab, Kai yawned. He'd been up all night, and riding in cars tended to make him sleepy anyway. He wished he could stretch his legs, but jammed between Sean and

Pat there was hardly any room. Kai tilted his head back against the seat and closed his eyes.

As usual before he fell asleep, memories of Hawaii came to him. Mostly the last place he and his mom had lived—Hanalei on the north shore of the island of Kauai. Hanalei was a lush green village made up of low wooden houses and buildings, as pretty and easygoing a place as you ever saw. Also a place where, every winter, one could find awesome swells and some of the longest-lasting and hollowest barrels anywhere on earth. Few thirteen-year-olds had as much tube time in those barrels as Kai had. But that, too, was in the past, and part of a memory that was still too painful to think about.

Eyes closed, a fog of sleep beginning to descend around him, Kai heard the rustle of the paper road map being folded. Then Pat spoke. "I think you boys are gonna like our next home. Looks like we're headed for Sun Haven."

Kai opened his eyes slightly. *Sun Haven?* It sounded sort of familiar, but in his drowsy state he couldn't quite remember where he'd heard that name before. Maybe in a surfing maga-zine? He closed his eyes again. No such luck.

Four

They drove for days, stopping now and then so Sean could sleep, eating cheap greasy food, breathing car exhaust and Pat's secondhand smoke. The floor of the truck cab was ankle deep with empty paper coffee cups, straws, napkins, and general road trip trash. Sean and Pat were incapable of throwing garbage out. Instead it piled up wherever they dropped it. Kai's body felt stiff and achy. He wished he could run, do some push-ups, whatever, just to get the blood flowing again.

He slept on and off, day and night, mostly out of boredom. A highway was a highway, light or dark. Cars, trucks, mile markers, signs, exit and entrance ramps. Not the most beautiful parts of God's green earth. Sometimes he didn't even bother looking any farther than the grimy, bug-splattered windshield. He'd play a game of trying to guess what color the guts of the next bug would be. Yellow, green, or red were generally winners. Clear was always interesting.

Early one morning he opened his eyes and something was different. They were no longer on the highway. Instead they were on an empty two-lane road with wisps of gray haze drifting across the pavement. To the left the road was lined with low, scrubby pines. Here and there a gnarled, leafless tree trunk with twisted, stubby wind-shorn branches rose up through the mist like a ghostly skeleton. To the right were tall sand dunes covered with long wavy dune grass. A seagull glided past.

Kai sat up and rubbed his eyes. The truck's cab felt cool and damp. Traces of salt air seeped in. They were near the ocean. Pat was asleep, his head wedged against the passenger-side window, his mouth open, his jaw covered with two or three days' worth of gray stubble. Kai gazed past him and out the window. Through the gaps in the sand dunes he caught glimpses of the ocean, dark gray-green beneath the early-morning cloud cover.

There were waves out there. Sets. Broad dark horizontal bands of water rolling in from the horizon. What had Pat said? They were going to Sun Haven? Kai didn't take his eyes off those passing dunes. Here and there through a gap, he saw a wave curling, a crash and explosion of white foam. He was tempted to tell Sean to stop the truck right there so he could get out and climb over the dunes, breathe that salt air, go down to the beach, and feel his feet sink into the sand, maybe even throw himself into the water.

But then the bad memories came back. No, maybe it wasn't such a good idea. And this was the wrong time to bring it up anyway. When Pat sensed there was something you really wanted, nothing made him happier than making sure you couldn't have it.

Next to him, the Alien Frog Beast stirred. Opened his eyes, squeezed them shut, then opened them again. "Where are we?"

"Pretty close, I think," Sean answered.

Pat rubbed his eyes and yawned without covering his mouth. His teeth were yellow and cruddy. It occurred to Kai that in the two years they'd been on the road together, most of that time living in the same room, he'd never actually seen the man brush his teeth. Pat reached into his shirt pocket and took out his glasses and a hard pack of Marlboros. He flipped open the top and pulled out a bent, half-smoked butt. With cigarettes costing so much these days, he rarely smoked one all at once.

He lit the butt and took a deep drag, exhaled and went into a spasm of coughing and cursing. Kai resisted the urge to roll his eyes. Every morning it was the same thing. Wake up, light a butt, cough his brains out. Pat rolled down the window. Kai felt a gust of cool damp salt air against his face while Pat hocked a loogie and rolled the window back up.

Big Chief Hockaloogie, Kai thought.

They started to pass wooden-framed beach houses on stilts with weather-beaten decks, and yards with rusty bicycles and cars and boats. Then a one-story gray shack with some orange fishing buoys and netting on the wall, and a couple of surfboards leaning against a fence. Except for surfing magazines and his small stash of videos, Kai hadn't seen a board in two years. He was caught off guard by the longing he suddenly felt, and forced it away. A lot of memories were coming back, and he didn't want to think about them right now.

They began to pass motels and gas stations and strip malls with beach shops and seafood restaurants and pizzerias. The sun started glinting here and there between the clouds. A big carved wooden sign on the side of the road said WELCOME TO SUN HAVEN.

"What do you want to do?" Sean asked.

"Drive into the middle of town," Pat said. "We'll check it out."

The restaurants got more elegant looking, the stores bigger, and the motels fancier, with lots of polished brass and maroon canopies and planters filled with flowers. There was something different about this town, and for a few moments Kai couldn't figure out what it was. Then it hit him—there were no fast-food places. No McDonald's, Burger Kings, Wendy's, Pizza Huts, Taco Bells.

Then oddly, just a block from what seemed like the busiest part of town, they passed a large, rundown beachfront motel. A two-story pink stucco structure with gray concrete patches on the walls and a red roof missing shingles here and there. A couple of broken windows were taped over with silver duct tape, and curly flakes of blue paint peeled from the wooden doors. A large sun-faded sign in front proclaimed it to be the Driftwood Motel, and leaning against the sign was an old yellowed long board with the words LOW RATES—SURFERS WELCOME painted on it. Unlike the other motels they'd passed, whose parking lots were crowded with shiny new cars, the Driftwood's lot was filled with a collection of dull, dented, rusted-out vehicles, a number of which had surfing stickers on the windows and bumpers, and a variety of surf racks on the roofs, some no more than towels wrapped in duct tape to keep them in place.

Sean brought the truck to a stop at what Kai sensed was the main intersection of town. A bank stood on one corner, a fancy seafood restaurant on another, but what caught Kai's eye was the long one-story building with large display windows filled with surfboards, bodyboards, beachwear, rafts, T-shirts, chairs, umbrellas, and just about anything else you could imagine taking to the shore. The sign said SUN HAVEN SURF, and the glass front door was covered with so many surf stickers that you couldn't see through it to what was inside.

"Hungry?" Pat asked.

Kai realized he was starving. "Yeah."

"Me too," said Sean.

Pat pointed through the bug-splattered windshield at a diner in the middle of the next block. "There's a place."

Sean drove down the block and eased the truck into a parking spot, and they got out. Standing on the sidewalk, Kai felt stiff and filled with pent up energy that begged to be burned off. The air smelled salty and felt damp and reminded him of early mornings in Hawaii, only here the fragrance of flowers was replaced by the scent of bacon. They went into the diner and were immediately eyeballed by the waitresses and most of the people sitting in the booths. Kai realized it was too early for the tourists to be up, so these were probably the locals. No doubt they were staring because Kai and his father and half brother—each of them unshaven, clothes wrinkled, hair askew— looked like something the cat dragged in.

Making no attempt to hide a glower of disapproval, a waitress with a blond ponytail and an armful of menus asked, "Smoking or nonsmoking?"

"Smoking," Pat said, and coughed without covering his mouth.

The waitress wrinkled her nose. "Good choice."

She showed them to a booth in the back of the diner, where they were less likely to be seen by clean-cut tourist families with kids, and handed them some menus. Kai noticed that the framed photos on the walls included some of surfers in tubes or catching air off some nicely shaped waves. The photos looked amateur, which made Kai think that those tubes and waves were someplace close by. Higher on the walls, above the height where you'd hang photos and paintings, hung surfboards, each with a small sign saying AVAILABLE AT SUN HAVEN SURF.

The waitress came by and filled their coffee cups. Sean studied the menu. Kai gazed at the surfboards. Pat lit a cigarette and began thumbing through one of the local newspapers he'd picked up on the way in.

The routine never varied. By the time they finished breakfast, he'd have picked out half a dozen ads for vacant storefronts in town. It was the week before Memorial Day and any landlord with a vacant store was in serious danger of missing the three biggest and most important months of the year—June through

August—when stores in this seaside town did ninety percent of their yearly business. A landlord in that position was likely to be desperate enough to agree to "flexible" terms about things like security deposits and rent.

That kind of desperation was just what Kai's father was counting on. By lunchtime he'd have the appointments lined up with the real estate brokers, as well as a bank account and a post office box under whatever new *South Park* name he was going by. (Kai's father had never tried the last name of Broflovski, mainly, Kai suspected, because he wasn't sure how to spell it.) By dinnertime he'd have a signed lease on a storefront. After dinner they'd start moving in. It would take all night. By tomorrow morning—even before the sign painter arrived, and while they were still putting out merchandise—the new T-shirt shop would be open for business.

Five

Nearly a week passed before Kai got any time off. It took that long to get the shelves and counters up, and the merchandise properly displayed. All the stock transfers had to be hung on the walls, and he and Sean had to take the truck to New York City to pick up supplies—everything from additional shelving to garments to the long fluorescent bulbs that lit the store.

Finally the store was up and running. Just as Kai's father had to have a new name in each new town, so did the shop. Pat had had shops named Total T, Happy T, T Time, Ts for 2s (and up), and Sweet T. The new store was clearly a master stroke: T-licious. Since tourists rarely got going before 10 A.M., that's when the store would open (and it would stay open until 10 P.M. and sometimes later), which meant that Kai could have the early mornings to himself.

The sun had not yet come up when his eyes opened. Through the small window at the back of the store Kai could see the last few bright stars disappearing into the dull grayness of the predawn. The only reason he was awake so early was because of Pat's loud snoring. Usually Kai could pull a pillow over his head and go back to sleep. But this morning it was no use. All week he'd been torn—tempted by the thought of the ocean being so close after two years of not seeing it. But at the same time dreading the memories it brought.

Memories. Kai knew he couldn't change what had happened. Things that were gone now and would never return. But the ocean was there. Today, tomorrow, and as long as he stayed in Sun Haven.

In the storeroom/office in the back of the shop, Kai quietly got up from the cheap plastic raft that served as his mattress. Officially and according to the lease, they were not allowed to live in the store, but they often did for the first few weeks after moving to a new town. While Pat was always in a rush to get the store running and earning money, he wasn't nearly as eager to start paying rent on a lousy apartment or some rooms in a boardinghouse.

Sean and Pat were still asleep on their rafts. Kai yawned and stretched. Standing now, he could see the eastern sky beginning to lighten as the sun started its daily ascent. He pulled on some shorts and a sweatshirt and started toward the back door, then stopped. He no longer owned a bathing suit, at least, not one that fit. An extra pair of boxers would have to do. And as far as a towel was concerned, he'd use one of the odd T-shirts that occasionally got messed up in the hot press and had to be tossed.

Kai quietly opened the back door and slipped out into the small parking lot behind the store. The dawn air was cool and fresh. He could smell the ocean. The cloudless sky was turning blue. A shiver ran through him as if to throw off the remains of cozy warm sleep. Then a long-forgotten sound reached his ears—in the early stillness of the morning came the distant crash of waves.

Kai started down the sidewalk and turned the corner onto the street that led to the beach. Except for the occasional car or delivery truck, the streets were empty. His view of the beach was blocked by a boardwalk, and as he walked toward it, the crashing of the waves gradually grew louder, bringing back those memories of the time when he was happy, when his mom was still alive and they lived in Hanalei.

Kai stopped near a row of parking meters. With those memories came a pain that was almost physical. But what was he supposed to do? Pretend the ocean wasn't there? Go back to the shop and hide? That was ridiculous. Sooner or later he had to face it.

He started walking again. Now, in addition to the waves, he could hear seagulls squawking. The smell of salt spray was in his nose. The sidewalk ended at the boardwalk. Kai climbed up the wooden ramp and crossed to the rail on the far side. There he stopped. Before him the Atlantic spread out like a vast gray-green blanket, the water glassy smooth except for the sets of south swells rolling in and crashing into white over a submerged sandbar forty yards offshore. The ocean, the water, the waves—Kai just stared. It had been a long time since he'd been this close. Suddenly the past two years felt like a bad, dry dream. And just like that, he knew he had to go in.

He went down the ramp to the beach, pulling off his shoes and letting his feet sink onto the cool early-morning sand. In the east the blue cloudless sky continued to brighten and the sun promised to be just a few minutes away from raising its sleepy head. A pair of seagulls swooped low and a tiny flock of sandpipers scampered at the water's foamy edge. The waves were small to medium, no more than chest high at best, but they were waves all the same, breaking cleanly right to left with very little sectioning. *A good day for long boarders,* Kai thought. A good day, period.

He walked past the tide mark and stopped. As his feet sank into the dark-colored wet sand he felt a shiver. The water was cold, almost icy. Kai took a few steps back and pulled his sweatshirt over his head. He stripped down to his boxers. The cool air made goose bumps rise on his skin. The orange sun was just peeking over the horizon, its rays still too weak to have any warming effect. Kai took a deep breath, and then bolted for the water.

There was no other way to get into surf this cold. You just had to throw your sorry butt in. Kai dove, and felt the frigid jolt against his skin as he slid under. His muscles instantly tightened. Damn, it was chilly. But rather than come up for air, he stayed under the surface and kicked. After two years on land, the sensation of gliding through liquid was irresistible. The wetness on his face and skin. The feeling of floating. Kai swam underwater until his lungs started to hurt and he felt the beginnings of an ice-cream headache. Then he stood up, his feet on the sandy bottom. As soon as his wet skin was exposed to the dawn air, he was chilled anew. By now his teeth were chattering and his hands were trembling, but there was one more thing he had to do before he went back to the beach and dried off. He looked out at the waves. A nice little inside set was coming from the sand bar. Kai felt the backwash tug at his legs, then dove ahead of the wave and kicked. The wave caught him. He stretched his right arm out and left arm back and felt his head pop out of the curl. He was riding again. Gliding in the frigid cold energy of the wave as it rolled toward the shore. The indescribable sensation of being carried in the pocket. How could he have forgotten how good it felt?

In the shallows the wave dropped him gently on the sand. Shivering, his teeth chattering, Kai stood up and let the seawater drip off. His skin was covered with goose bumps. The cool morning air offered no comfort. He jogged back to his clothes and used the extra T-shirt to wipe himself down. The beach was empty and he was tempted to just kick his wet boxers off and pull on the dry pair, but you never knew who might be watching. So he wrapped the damp T-shirt around his waist, pulled the wet boxers down and the dry ones up. He was still shivering as he pulled on his shorts and sweatshirt. One thing was for sure—he was going to have to get a wet suit if he was ever going to surf here.

He squeezed as much seawater out of the boxers as he could and then walked back up the beach and dropped the wet T-shirt in a garbage can made from a green fifty-gallon drum. He was about to head back to the boardwalk when out of the corner of his eye, he noticed something he'd missed before. A few hundred yards down the beach was a jetty made of huge blocks of stone. The waves appeared larger there, curling more top to bottom with a bit more snap. Some were small barrels. But what really caught Kai's attention were the two people out there surfing. Kai was certain they hadn't been there when he'd arrived. They must have come while he was in the water.

Curious, Kai walked down the beach toward them. Both were wearing black wet suits. As Kai got closer he could see that one of the surfers was young with blond hair, probably around his age, riding a short board. The other, an older man who also had blond hair, was sitting just outside the takeoff zone, also on a short board. The younger guy would catch a wave, carve a turn, try to get some air, whatever, then paddle back and talk it over with the older guy.

Kai stopped and watched as the kid worked on the same maneuver—a frontside air—over and over. The angle of attack never varied. No matter how the wave broke it was the same thing. In Kai's estimation this wasn't surfing. It was drill practice. The kid was good, there was no arguing that, but Kai had seen that style before. It wasn't about riding a wave, it was about beating it into submission, shredding it as if the wave wasn't something to enjoy, but rather something to destroy. It was a competitive style designed to impress judges and crowds of grommets. And the manufacturers of sneakers and sunglasses who needed cool-looking young surfer dudes to endorse their products.

To Kai it represented the Dark Ages of surfing. Something so foreign to the original idea of the sport, that he wondered if the ancient Hawaiians would even be able to comprehend what he was looking at.

He watched for a moment more, then turned away and headed back up the beach. Originally he'd hoped to stay in the water longer, but that was not an option. It was just too cold. Instead he decided to check out the Driftwood Motel, where there were low rates and surfers were welcome.

Six

Kai couldn't explain exactly what it was that made him curious about the Driftwood. Maybe because it was the only place around that reminded him of Hawaii. Almost every other building in Sun Haven was new and shiny and polished. But the Driftwood appeared to be that rare and unique place that was not in the business of profiting off surfers, but rather in the business of helping them do the thing they loved to do.

Since the boardwalk didn't go very far in either direction, Kai decided to walk down the beach to the motel. By now a few older beachcombers were out, ambling along the water's edge with sticks and sorting through the jumbles of seaweed and other debris that had washed up during the night. Kai himself stopped here and there to pick up a shell, or interesting-looking rock. He was amused by the sun-whitened nuggets of surf wax scattered here and there on the sand, along with a torn leash from a bodyboard, and a tattered wet suit bootie. All evidence that a lot of surfing took place along these shores.

Down the beach, about two hundred yards past the end of the boardwalk, two surfers in full wet suits came through an opening in the dunes carrying long boards. Kai watched enviously as they stopped near the water's edge and crouched over their boards for a quick wax up, then broke into a sprint and launched themselves and their boards into the water and began paddling. He walked toward the grass-covered dunes they'd come through, wondering if this was the way to and from the Driftwood Motel.

The path he found through the tall bushes and scrub pines was well worn. A mixture of sand, gravel, and random patches of grass and weeds. It curved so that you couldn't see what was ahead. Kai walked slowly and alertly, just in case he was trespassing and there was a dog around with a heightened sense of territoriality.

He came around a large, thick green bush and found himself standing in the backyard of the two-story pink motel building, its second-floor railing barely visible under the rows of colorful towels, wet suits, and rash guards left out overnight to dry. But that wasn't what Kai focused on. What he saw instead were hundreds of surfboards. Mostly long boards, and they were everywhere. Propped up against the tall wooden fence that ran around the perimeter of the yard. Leaning against the shed in the back of the yard. Angled onto an old wooden picnic table. Another twenty or thirty were leaning against a tree, forming what looked like a big Indian tepee.

Kai couldn't believe his eyes. It was as if he'd died and gone to surfboard heaven. Or maybe a surfboard junkyard, since when he gave the boards a closer look, he saw that most were damaged in one way or another. Either badly dinged, or sun yellowed and water-logged, a fin broken off and missing, a deck delaminating. He'd wandered into a surfboard orphanage.

Still, even if the boards weren't in great shape, they had history. Thousands of waves ridden. Tubes. Decks walked. Toes on the nose. Kai ran his fingers over the smooth deck of a nine-and-a-half-foot square-tail Gordon & Smith with the fin broken off. A lot of the boards were custom jobs with names Kai had never heard of, but they looked good, with nice rails and sloping rockers. These boards might have been old and damaged, but they weren't junk. And whoever had collected them knew what he was doing, or at least had good taste. Kai found a beautiful Town & County with the nose bashed in. Too bad. There was something interesting behind it. He had to move a few boards out of the way, and there it was—a nine-foot Trigger Brothers. White with sky blue rails. Even out in Hawaii, Kai had heard stories about these Australian shapers and their amazing boards. What in the world was a Trigger Brothers stick doing here on the east coast of the United States, probably fifteen thousand miles from its home?

"Help you with somethin'?" a gravely voice asked.

Kai turned around. About twenty feet away stood a man wearing ripped jeans, a faded green Hawaiian shirt, and a sun-blasted blue baseball cap. It was hard to tell how old he was. Maybe Pat's age. Maybe older. His skin was rough and lined and tan despite it being early summer. But what was unmistakable was the sawed-off double-barreled shotgun in his hands—aimed straight at Kai.

Seven

"**Y**ou don't have to aim that at me," Kai said. His arms were at his sides, but he held his hands out, palms turned forward to show the man that he wasn't concealing any weapons.

"Well, that's very kind of you to tell me what I don't have to do," the man said, his voice as rough and worn as the boards around them. "But I think I'll do it anyway. Now let me ask you a question. Would you be aware that this is private property you're standing on?"

Kai nodded.

"You wouldn't happen to be familiar with the word *trespassing* now would you?" the man asked.

"I was just admiring the boards," Kai said.

"Well, I suppose I could see that," the man said. "Only, in order to admire these boards you had to cross about twenty-five yards of private property. Now let me ask you another question. You know why they call it *private* property?"

"Because it's private."

The man smiled. "Well, you are a sharp young fellow, aren't you. And I bet you know that word *private* means you shouldn't be here."

"Where'd you get that Trigger Brothers board?" Kai asked.

The man scowled and lowered the gun slightly. "I know you?"

Kai shook his head.

"You're not from around here?"

"Nope."

"So . . . if you're not from around here, what are you doing here?"

"Just moved in," Kai said.

"And where would that be from?"

"Here and there. The last place I really called home was Hawaii."

The man's bushy eyebrows rose. "No kiddin'?" Just as fast as his eyebrows had risen, they now dipped with suspicion. Once again Kai found the sawed-off shotgun aimed at his midsection.

"So tell me, where in Hawaii would you call home?"

"Hanalei, on the north shore of—"

"Kauai," the man with the gun finished the sentence for him. "Who sells the best shave ice?"

"I could argue that with you," Kai said.

The man nodded down at the shotgun. "And with all due respect, I could pull the trigger and blow off both your legs. And when the police asked me what happened, I would probably say that this young stranger tried to attack and rob me."

"Most people will tell you Jo-Jo's has the best shave ice," Kai said. "But I like Wishing Well."

"Not a goddamn chance in hell." The man grinned. "But being from Hanalei, I expect you would say that. So how'd you wind up here?"

"That's a long story," Kai said. "I'd be glad to tell you, but it's a little hard to concentrate with that gun aimed at me."

"Why? You got ADD or something?"

"No," Kai replied. "I've got DWTD. As in Don't Want To Die."

The man smirked and tossed the gun toward the grass. Kai instantly ducked. Dropped firearms had a way of going off unexpectedly.

"Don't look so concerned," said the man. "It's broke and it ain't even loaded."

"Thanks for telling me," Kai said, his heart still pounding in his chest.

The man stepped toward him and held out his hand. "My name's Curtis. What's yours?"

"Kai." They shook hands.

"Kai? Like in ocean?"

"Yeah. My mom named me that."

"Well, Kai, welcome to Sun Haven." The old man seemed to focus on Kai's head. He reached forward and picked off a thin sliver of green translucent seaweed. "You already been in the water this morning?"

Kai nodded.

"A bit cold, huh?"

"It's been a long time since I had the chance."

Curtis looked as if he was studying him, or seeing inside. It made Kai uncomfortable. He jerked his head back toward the boards. "So what's with the Trigger Brothers?"

Curtis grinned. "I acquired that stick from Phil Trigger himself."

"In Australia?" Kai asked.

"Damn right. Surfed that board over most of the South Pacific before you were even born." Curtis narrowed one eye at him. "You wouldn't happen to drink coffee, would you?"

Kai nodded.

"Well, you shouldn't," Curtis said. "Lousy habit. Probably stunt your growth. How do you like it?"

"Uh, milk and sugar."

"Fair enough, be right back." With a slight limp, Curtis headed back around the side of the motel. As soon as he was out of sight, Kai went over and picked up the sawed-off shotgun. It felt ominously heavy. Kai opened the breech. Inside were the dull brass ends of two shells. *Unloaded, huh?* Kai shook the shells out, closed the breech, cocked the gun, and pulled the trigger. He heard a loud, hollow click. While he wasn't a firearms expert, it sure as heck seemed to him that the gun worked fine. He slid the two shells back into the chambers, closed the breech, and placed the gun gently back on the ground.

Up on the second floor of the motel, a

door opened and a sleepy-faced thin guy with tousled blond hair stepped out. The sun was getting higher now, and the guy shielded his eyes and squinted out over the dunes toward the water. He had tattoos on both arms and looked like he was in his twenties. The only thing he was wearing was a pair of dull orange boxers and a hemp necklace.

"How's it look?" someone inside the room asked.

"Okay, nothing great," the guy with the tousled hair called back.

"It's better down by the jetty," Kai said.

The guy squinted down at Kai as if noticing him for the first time. "You mean, Screamers?"

"That what they call it?" Kai asked.

The guy nodded.

"Looked like you might even get tubed," Kai said.

The guy grinned, but there was a nasty glint in his eye. "You think so?"

"Who you talkin' to?" called the voice from within the room.

"Kid says we could probably get tubed down at Screamers," the guy with the tousled hair said in a wry tone.

A stocky guy with dark hair shaved close to his head came out onto the balcony. He had a beer can in his hand and black tattoos on both shoulders. He stared down at Kai. "*You* ever get tubed down at Screamers?"

"I just moved here," Kai said. "Don't even have a surfboard yet."

The dark-haired guy snorted and turned to his friend. "So what do you want to do?"

"Go back to sleep and hope it gets bigger later." The blond guy went back into the room. The dark-haired guy took a gulp of beer and gazed down at Kai for a moment. Then he let out a loud belch and followed his friend, slamming the door closed behind him.

Eight

Curtis came around the side of the motel carrying two mugs of coffee. "Here you go." He handed Kai a chipped green mug with vague traces of red lipstick on the rim. Kai seriously doubted Curtis had washed it out before filling it with coffee, but he took a sip anyway. The coffee was scalding and tasted good. And it felt good to be in the sun and feel its warming rays.

"Why don't you have yourself a seat." Curtis pulled over a rusty old beach chair held together with brown twine and duct tape. "Just ease on down slow, okay? Sometimes these chairs can't take the weight."

Kai settled gently into the chair. It creaked

and sagged, but didn't collapse. He was starting to get the feeling that everything Curtis owned was old, broken, and held together with rope and tape. Curtis pulled out a chair for himself and sat down. Kai caught a whiff of something unusual and couldn't place it for a moment. Then he realized it was whisky, coming from Curtis's mug. The old guy must've mixed his coffee with booze, and the vapor carried the scent.

Curtis took a sip, then lowered his mug and stared at patchy scars that ran the length of Kai's right leg from the thigh down to his ankle.

"Guy up on the second floor came out and looked at the waves," Kai said. "He was hoping they might get bigger later."

Curtis gazed toward the east. It almost seemed to Kai that he lifted his nose and sniffed the air. He shook his head. "Wouldn't hold my breath. It's gonna keep warming up all day. By this afternoon the onshore thermals'll kick in and blow everything out. By tonight the swell will be pretty much the same or a little less."

"You checked the forecast and the buoy reports?" Kai asked.

"Nope."

"Then how do you know?" Kai asked.

Curtis raised a finger to the side of his nose.

"You can smell the weather?" Kai said, half teasing.

Curtis leaned toward him. "Take a closer look."

On the side of the older man's nose was a faint circle about the size of a dime. The skin inside the circle was a slightly lighter color.

"You ever heard of a melanoma?" Curtis said. "Skin cancer. They've probably taken a dozen or two off my face, arms, and back. Know why? Because since the day I was born I've spent about every minute I could in the ocean. And the sun makes you pay dearly for that. But I know that ocean. I know what she's gonna do and when she's gonna do it."

"So what's tomorrow morning going to be like?" Kai asked.

Curtis gazed up at the clear blue sky for a moment. "Glassy, smaller, mostly knee high with a few bigger sets mixed in. They'll be real clean early, before the wind gets on it. Fun little waves."

"Think you'll go out?" Kai asked.

"For knee high?" Curtis shook his head. "But you would, right? You'd be out there in mush and ankleslappers if you could."

Kai shrugged, but they both knew that was true.

"So let's get back to your story," Curtis said. "You were gonna tell me how you wound up here."

"My mom died and they sent me stateside to live with my dad. He tends to move around a lot."

"Oh, yeah? What's he do?"

"Runs T-shirt shops. The kind where you get to create your own shirt."

"How come he moves around so much?"

Kai shrugged. No way he could tell the truth. "He just likes to."

Curtis studied him again. "Is that so?"

Kai nodded at the sawed-off shotgun lying in the grass. "Thought you said it was unloaded and broken."

Curtis raised an eyebrow. "Did I? Well, I guess that makes us both a couple of liars."

Kai took a last sip of his coffee. This Curtis guy seemed to know more about him than he liked. "It's getting late. I gotta go to work."

"Where?" Curtis asked.

"T-shirt shop. For my dad." Kai put the coffee mug down on the grass and stood up. "Thanks for the coffee . . . and for not shooting me."

"My pleasure," Curtis said.

"Well, see ya." Kai started back toward the path through the bushes.

"Son, can I ask you a question?" Curtis said.

Kai stopped. "Uh, sure."

"You got yourself a board?"

Kai shook his head.

"You gonna get one?"

"I don't know."

Curtis gave him a look. The same way he looked at the sky and decided what the weather would be. "But you want one bad, don't you?"

"Maybe." Kai felt uncomfortable. It was one thing to go back into the ocean again. But to get back on a board. That would be something else.

"Maybe it's a money thing," Curtis guessed, this time only half right. "Your dad pay you for the work you do in that T-shirt shop?"

"Just pocket money. He says whatever I'd

earn in the shop is what he pays for my room and board."

Curtis rubbed his stubbled chin. "Well, then, wait a second." He hefted himself out of his chair and started toward the backyard shed. He took a ring of keys out of his pocket and unlocked the door.

"Come on in here," he said, pulling open the doors. It was dim and damp inside. The only light came from some translucent plastic panels in the roof. It smelled like neoprene wet suits and surf wax. Kai stood at the entrance and waited for his eyes to adjust. The walls of the shed were lined with racks filled with boards. Almost all between eight and ten feet. Kai had a feeling this was Curtis's private quiver. A light blue Bruce Jones. A banana yellow Rennie Yater. A plain off-white Rusty. Some custom boards with no markings whatsoever. A bunch of wet suits were hanging on pegs against the back wall. Curtis held one up, looking back and forth between Kai and the suit. He seemed to make a decision, and tossed it to Kai. Then he came back out of the shed and relocked it.

"Now let's see if we can find you a board," he said.

No, Kai thought, *I'm not ready to deal with this.*

But Curtis couldn't hear Kai's thoughts. The older man started toward the tree where the boards formed that Indian tepee. Kai stood wordlessly, the wet suit draped over his arm. He couldn't quite believe this was happening, but he couldn't quite muster the words to stop it either. The guy couldn't just be giving him a board. There had to be a price to pay.

Curtis went through some boards. "I'd say given the size of the waves you're gonna see for the rest of the week, and the fact that you haven't surfed in a while . . ." He stopped and gazed at a sun-yellowed nine-footer with a red single fin and several large white patches indicating some major ding repairs, including one where the leash plug used to be. "You okay without a leash?"

"What are you doing?" Kai asked.

Curtis stiffened slightly. "I'm giving you what you need, son."

Kai caught a whiff of the older man's breath and realized he'd had a lot more to drink than the whisky in his coffee. And it wasn't even 9 A.M. yet.

"I don't need this," Kai said. "I don't even want it."

"You don't, huh? I suppose next you're gonna tell me you hate being in the water. That's why you went in without a wet suit this morning and froze your young butt off. And I suppose you don't like to surf, either. That's why I found you out here, caressing my boards like they were some kind of religious idols. That's why you know who the Trigger Brothers are, and about buoy reports and asked what I thought the surf would be like tomorrow morning. That's why you lost half the skin on your right leg on a patch of coral somewhere and are probably lucky you didn't die from the staph infection that followed. All because you hate the doggone ocean and you hate surfing."

Kai stared down at the weeds and grass, the old cigarette butts and plastic rings from six packs.

Curtis leaned the sun-yellowed board toward him. "Look, son, I'm doing you a favor here. Didn't anyone ever tell you not to look a gift horse in the mouth?"

"So what do you want in return?" Kai asked.

"What do I want in return?" Curtis repeated. "Not much. Just everything you have."

"I don't have anything," Kai said.

"Exactly."

It took Kai a moment. "You serious?"

"Aloha, grommet. Now go out and enjoy yourself."

Kai took the board by the rails. The second it was in his hands, he knew he was hooked. There was no way he could refuse. He wasn't sure what felt more uncomfortable—accepting such valuable gifts from a stranger, or the way this semidrunk shaman seemed to know him better than he knew himself. "I don't know when I'll be able to pay you."

"I say anything about getting paid?" Curtis asked. "Christ, grommet, don't you get it? Just bring it back when you're done." He walked back across the yard, bent down and picked up the saw-off shotgun. Kai still hadn't moved. This whole thing felt too weird. Like a dream come true, only it was a dream he had not allowed himself to have. Curtis stared at him. "Something wrong?"

"No," Kai said. "I . . . I just want to say thanks. This means a lot to me."

"Damn straight, it does," Curtis said. "Why the hell you think I did it?"

Nine

It was easier than he might have imagined to walk back down the beach with the board and wet suit and still resist surfing—a condition he attributed mostly to the shock he was feeling over what had just happened at the Driftwood. It was totally possible, maybe even probable, that sooner or later he would have reached this point by himself and decided to find a board and a wet suit. But that should have taken months, not days or weeks. Then again, months from now would be the fall and then winter. So again, maybe Curtis knew something Kai didn't know.

Anyway, going surfing now would probably mean being late for work, and the Alien Frog

Beast was liable to go ballistic and break the board in half. Speaking of the board, now that Kai had had time to take a closer look, he could see that it was a beauty. Custom shaped by someone who knew what he was doing. The only markings were the number *43* and the initials *TL* on the stringer. On the negative side, Kai could tell from the weight that the old stick had some water inside her. Likewise, the wet suit was an old Body Glove with restitched seams and bagged-out knees. But beggars couldn't be choosers. Or what had Curtis said? Something about a horse's mouth?

As Kai walked back along the beach he saw that there were more surfers in the water now. He couldn't help but feel a little envious while they paddled out and caught waves he knew he could be riding. But along with it came a lot of feelings that he wasn't sure what to do with. In a way, he was glad when he got to the parking lot and turned away from the beach and toward town.

He was crossing the lot when he noticed the bright yellow Hummer and the two surfers stripping off their wet suits. Kai knew at once that they were the two he'd seen earlier by the jetty, surfing the spot called Screamers. Seeing them up close now, he was willing to bet that they were father and son. They had the same broad-shouldered build, the same shape and look of face, the same reddish blond hair, although the father's was streaked with gray. As they pulled off their wet suits and toweled their heads, both were grim and tight lipped, the way people looked after an argument. It was difficult for Kai to imagine what they could possibly be unhappy about, unless it was related to having to stop surfing on such a beautiful day.

Neither seemed to notice Kai as he passed. Father and son were silent, not even looking at each other. Finally the younger one climbed in on the passenger side of the Hummer, slamming the door so hard the whole vehicle shook. The father got in next, started the SUV, and turned out of the lot. Only then did Kai notice the license plate: SUNSURF.

Kai left the parking lot and started down the sidewalk. The sun felt warm on his head and shoulders. A young woman—Kai guessed she might be in her early twenties—was coming toward him carrying a long board with a red-and-black wet suit draped over it. She was wearing a hooded gray sweatshirt and had short black hair and blue eyes. As they got closer, she stopped.

"How is it?" she asked.

"At best medium, but pretty clean," he said.

"Sometimes that's all you can ask for around here." She held his eyes with hers a second longer than necessary, then flashed him a bright white smile. "Catch you down there sometime?"

"Uh, sure."

She continued toward the beach and he walked toward the shop. It was weird how that seemed to happen more and more often lately. Not just with girls his own age, but with women who appeared to be five or even ten years older. His mom used to tease him that once he'd had his growth spurt he'd become irresistible, that women would lose themselves in the oceanic depths of his blue eyes. But then she died and wasn't there to decide whether her prediction had come true.

Kai cut through the parking lot behind the T-shirt shop. It was almost 10 A.M. and the streets were starting to fill with traffic. The sidewalks were getting crowded with shoppers and beachgoers. Behind the shop Kai leaned the board carefully against the wall beside the back door, then let himself in. The air inside smelled of coffee and cigarettes.

"Where you been?" his father asked when Kai walked into the office/sleeping area. Both Pat and Sean were sitting on some cheap plastic beach chairs they'd picked up the previous day in Wal-Mart. Pat was staring at his computer. Sean was reading a comic book.

"Went for a walk," Kai said.

"Did I say you could do that?" Pat asked.

"Didn't say I couldn't."

"What's that?" Pat pointed at the wet suit Curtis had given Kai.

"It's a wet suit," Kai answered.

"Where'd you get it?"

"Someone gave it to me."

Pat smirked. "Right. You were just walking along and someone handed it to you. So what'd you do? Find it in the garbage, or steal it?"

"I told you what happened," Kai said.

His father held out his hand. "Let me see it."

"No."

Before Kai could react, Pat grabbed it. The frog-eyed alien could be deceptively fast. Pat held it up by the arms as if trying to figure out how it worked.

"You gonna go diving?" Sean asked.

"It's for surfing, you retard," Pat said in an awesome display of paternal affection. "Haven't you ever noticed those dumb magazines sonny boy wastes his money on?"

Pat tossed the wet suit back to Kai, at the same time giving him a close look. "Won't do you much good if you don't have a surfboard."

Kai hesitated. "Maybe I do," he said.

Pat was quiet for a moment. Behind the thick glasses his eyes narrowed as he considered what Kai had said. "Where'd you get a surfboard?"

Kai didn't answer.

"Where is it?" Pat asked.

"Outside against the back wall."

With a sour look on his face, Pat heaved himself out of the chair and went through the back door. Kai followed, just in case his father decided to try something stupid. Outside, the sun was high and bright. Just as Curtis had predicted, the day was starting to warm up. Pat stood with his hands on his hips, staring at the board.

"I suppose someone gave you this, too," he said.

"Matter of fact, yes," Kai said.

Pat spun on him. "What do you take me for, a fool? Who the hell you know in this town would give you a wet suit and a board just like that?"

"Someone who understands things you'll never understand."

Pat's face turned red and he pointed a nicotine-stained finger at Kai. "Listen to me, you wiseass little punk, you get rid of this stuff right now, understand? I can't have the cops sniffing around here looking for stolen property, and I sure as hell can't have them finding any."

The irony of this statement was not lost on Kai, who was well aware that just about everything in his father's shop was stolen property, although Pat was inclined to say that it simply hadn't been paid for . . . yet.

And never would be.

"I told you the truth," Kai said. "It's not stolen property. Someone gave it to me. And I'm not getting rid of it."

"If you won't, then I will." Pat reached toward the board.

"You touch that board and I'll . . ." Kai didn't finish the sentence.

Pat looked up. "You'll what?"

"Don't touch it," Kai said.

Pat stared at him with a firm, set jaw. Then, unexpectedly, he started to smile. "Okay, tough guy, but the cops come around asking questions, I'm gonna tell them exactly what you told me. Then it'll be up to you to explain how you got this stuff."

"Fine with me," Kai said.

As if he was only now becoming aware that he was outside in the parking lot, Pat squinted up at the hot yellow sun and wiped some sweat off his forehead. "Lord, I hate that damn sun," he muttered, and went back inside.

Kai stood outside a moment longer, gazing at the old yellowed board, and feeling a smile grow on his face and the heat of the sun bake his shoulders. He was starting to like it here.

Ten

"Good day, huh?" said the guy on the long board floating about a dozen feet away from Kai.

Kai nodded. "A little cold." Actually, he was freezing, shivering, his teeth chattering and his feet and hands numbed by the fifty-six-degree water. But the guy was right—it was a good day. Morning, really, considering it wasn't yet 8 A.M. Waist- to shoulder-high sets rolling in against an offshore breeze that kicked plumes of rainbow sea spray high over their heads. Considering how cold it was, had the conditions been anything less, Kai would have been back in the shop.

But now he had another reason to stay in

the frigid water. He'd been watching this guy all week. He was definitely older than Kai, but maybe not that much older. Tall and skinny with hunched shoulders, long black hair in a thick braid down his back, a wispy Fu Manchu mustache and a sort of goofy look, but sick flawless on the long board. He paddled out on his knees, and once on a wave he traipsed up and down the deck like a tightrope walker, sometimes getting toes on the nose going left, then scampering back for a classic drop knee turn, changing direction and getting back to the nose on an inside right.

"That a three-two?" the guy asked, looking at Kai's wet suit.

Kai nodded and shivered. The tall guy was wearing a pretty new-looking 4/3 Body Glove, booties, gloves, and a neoprene hood.

"Dude, no wonder you're cold," the guy said. "I'm wearing all this and I'm cold too."

Kai looked closer and saw that his lips were blue. Suddenly the guy's back straightened and he lifted his head. Kai knew he was watching a wave come in. He turned and looked. The crest of the first wave in a good-size set was visible behind the closer smaller waves. The first wave of the set, typically, was only a promise of bigger ones behind it. Both Kai and the guy turned their boards toward shore and watched over their shoulders. They let the first wave in the set roll beneath them. The second wave loomed up behind it, an A-frame and definitely one of the largest of the day, its peak almost dead center between Kai and the other guy, who was already paddling left.

Kai knew the right would be shorter, but he was ready to go in and this was definitely the wave to take. He started to paddle and felt the water draw tight under the board and back up the wave's face. The tail of the board lifted and he was up and planing across the glassy curl, keeping the board high in the wave as he walked it, getting a cheater five over the nose then arching way back, holding it as long as he could. Which wasn't very long. The wave closed out and Kai stepped back to the tail and swung the nose around, hoping for an inside left. It wasn't there and so he rode in on the soup. Fifty yards to his left, the other guy had decided to do the same thing.

Kai carried the board up the beach to the dry sand and sat down. The sun was rising up in the east, but the cool offshore breeze limited its warming rays. The other guy paused for a moment in the shallows to wrap the leash around the tail of his board, then walked up and sat down next to Kai.

"Great freakin' day if it wasn't so cold," the guy said.

"Yeah," Kai answered through chattering teeth.

"Where'd you learn to go switch foot like that?"

"Don't know," Kai said. "I just always could. Where'd you learn to walk a board like that?"

"From a book," the guy said, stripping off the gloves and rubbing his white, wrinkled hands together.

"Serious?"

"For sure. I used to sort of slide my feet up and back like everybody else, and then I was reading this book and it said the real way to walk the board was the cross-step. Like Wingnut did in *Endless Summer Two,* you know? The book said you can practice it anywhere, so for about a month I practiced walking the board wherever I was." The guy stood up and pretended to walk the board in the sand. "I'd do it on the sidewalk, in stores, at the library. You name it."

"Didn't people think you were kind of weird?" Kai asked.

"So what else is new?" The guy offered his hand to Kai. "I'm Bean."

"Kai." They shook hands.

"You new around here?" Bean asked.

Kai nodded.

"Where're you from?"

Kai explained that he was originally from Hawaii and had just bounced around from place to place since then.

"Hawaii, man," Bean said wistfully. "Average air temperature around seventy-eight degrees. Average water around seventy-five. You never need a wet suit."

"You've been there?" Kai said.

Bean shook his head. "Read about it."

Out at the break where they'd just been surfing, another set rolled in. Clearly there was some sort of deviation in the sea bottom at that spot, because the swells jacked up and peaked there pretty consistently.

"So that place where we were surfing, does it have a name?" Kai asked.

"Sewers."

"For real?"

"Yeah, the story is way back in the old

days they built a sewer line from the town out here. Can you believe it? I mean, they were trying to be a beach resort and at the same time they were pumping raw sewage into the ocean fifty yards offshore. Anyway, after a while the state told them they had to shut it down, so they did, but they just left what was out there. Under that spot where the waves break, there's a bunch of cement and pipes down under the sand. It's kind of funny how something bad turned out to be something good, you know?"

"Hey." A kid trotted up carrying a blue bodyboard and blue-and-yellow flippers. He had brownish hair and freckles and was wearing a shorty wet suit. Kai figured him for about thirteen or fourteen years old. "You guys been out? It looks rippin'."

"Be prepared to freeze your butt," Bean warned him. "Water's probably around fifty-five degrees this morning."

"One good ride and it'll be worth it," the kid said, and looked curiously at Kai.

"Booger, meet Kai," Bean said.

The freckled kid nodded at Kai. "Hey."

They heard loud hoots and looked down the beach. A small crowd of short boarders were riding near the jetty in the break they called Screamers. One of them was crouched down, hand on the rail in a small tube. Kai was not surprised to see that it was the same guy he'd seen out surfing with his father the week before. He and his crowd were there most mornings by 7 A.M. Kai had been watching them all week. They had that king-of-the-hill don't-mess-with-us attitude. Anytime an outsider got too close, they were seriously vibed. This being a resort town, a lot of surfers wouldn't be local. But even a surfer who'd never surfed there before knew the vibe when it was aimed at him, and knew to steer clear.

The guy who'd just gotten tubed finished his ride and kicked out, raising his hands in fists as he and his board sank in the trough.

"Lucas Frank," Bean said. "Local surf hero."

"His dad owns Sun Haven Surf," Booger said. "You ever hear of Buzzy Frank?"

Kai shook his head.

"They say he's the best surfer to ever come out of the northeast," Booger said.

"Not that it means much when you're going up against guys who surf Sebastian Inlet and Pipeline every day of the year," Bean added. "But he was on the pro tour for a while and kept up with some pretty heavy dudes. Then he came back here and used his rep to start Sun Haven Surf."

"And now Lucas and his friends think they own Screamers?" Kai asked.

"You have to ask?" Bean replied.

Locals. It was the same story everywhere. The brahs got together wherever the surf was the best and acted like they owned the break. Anyone else who tried to surf there got his ass kicked, either in the water or on the beach. Sometimes both. It was an old story, but one Kai knew all too well.

Kai stood up. "Tell you what. We get the same swell tomorrow morning, someone's going to have to go over there and pay them a visit."

Bean and Booger shared a look.

"I wouldn't do that," Bean said. "The local scene here is way heavy. I mean, you take your life in your hands."

"Too bad," said Kai.

"This I gotta see," said Booger.

Eleven

The next morning the conditions were pretty much the same—shoulder-high sets. The offshore breeze had died down a little and the waves were glassy. As Kai crossed the boardwalk in his wet suit with his board under his arm, he was surprised to find a small crowd down at the beach. He spotted Bean and Booger in the group and realized immediately what had happened—word had spread that Kai was planning to break into the Screamers lineup.

Kai instantly regretted that he'd said anything about it. The last thing he'd wanted was a big showdown. Out at Screamers there were at least half a dozen guys bobbing on boards in the water—twice the number that usually showed up at that time of day. This was all wrong. Kai had hoped to come down to an empty beach, paddle out to Screamers and just start catching waves. Being on a long board, he knew he could get on the wave a lot earlier than a short boarder. There was only one rule in surfing: First man up on his board closest to the peak had the right to the wave and everyone else was supposed to back off.

Kai knew the local guys in the Screamers lineup would "drop in" on him to test his resolve. But he believed that if he stood his ground and refused to give up the wave, the others would eventually let him into the lineup. But that might have happened if there were only two or three guys out at Screamers and no crowd on the beach. The presence of all these people upped the ante. Now there was too much of what the Japanese called face that had to be saved. If he went out now, there was a good chance someone would get hurt.

He stopped and lowered the tail of his board to the sand. He looked at the crowd of kids, almost all of them now looking back at him. With the exception of Bean and Booger, he wasn't sure he'd ever seen any of them before. He looked at the waves. He looked out at Screamers. A nice set was coming in, but not one of the locals was paddling to get into position. They, too, were all watching Kai.

The whole scene reminded Kai of some East Los Angeles turf war between rival drug gangs. This was definitely not what surfing was about. To paddle out to Screamers now was to incite everything he was against: unnecessary violence, localism, hate. Kai picked up his board and started back up the beach.

"Hey!" Booger came running up behind him. "Where you going?"

"Home," Kai answered.

"But you said you were gonna surf Screamers."

"I was," Kai said. "But I came here to surf, not to fight."

"But we told everybody," Booger said.

"It's nobody else's business."

"But they're waiting," said Booger.

"That's their problem," Kai said.

"So that's it? You're just gonna chicken out and go home?"

Kai stopped. Booger also stopped. The kid turned pale and his jaw dropped as if he'd just realized what he'd said.

"I . . . I didn't mean it like that."

Kai felt himself relax. You knew Booger was one of those kids you couldn't get angry with. He was simply a spongehead and a nerd, but he didn't have a mean bone in his body.

"What way did you mean it?" Kai asked.

"Just that . . . uh . . . uh."

"Uh, uh, uh?" Kai imitated him, then smiled. Booger went from pale to bright red. Kai wondered how many more colors he could turn.

"Listen," Kai said. "Just because it's over for today doesn't mean it's over. It's like catching waves. You gotta pick your spots."

"But what do I tell everyone?" Booger asked.

"Tell them . . ." Kai paused and thought. "Tell them to have a nice day."

"Huh?"

But it was too late. Kai was going home.

In the back room at T-licious, he changed out of his wet suit and helped himself to a couple of Pop-Tarts. Pat had already started smoking and coughing. The shop wouldn't open for an hour and a half and the last thing Kai wanted to do was spend any more time than necessary with Sean and Alien Frog

Chief Hockaloogie. So he went back out.

This time his destination was Sun Haven Surf, the store owned by Lucas Frank's father. The place had just opened for the day when Kai stepped through the surf sticker-covered front door. The first thing he noticed was the familiar smell of neoprene and surf wax. Driving guitar riffs were blaring out of the video monitors behind the counters. On the screens pumped-up surfers caught crazy airs and skittered down the faces of mountainous waves. Kai had seen so many surf movies that he could usually tell exactly where each scene was filmed. The shot of the guy being towed into a greenish gray four-story macker was definitely Maverick's. That heavy-lipped tube going square could only be Teahupoo. And any grom in the world could recognize the awesome curl of Pipeline long before it spit.

As Kai's eyes began to focus, he realized that this surf shop was unlike any he'd seen before. For one thing, except for the stacks of wax on the counter near the door, and the leashes, nose guards, and traction pads on the wall, there was almost nothing in this entire part of the store that applied to surfing. Instead, it was all surfing "related"—endless racks of

T-shirts and bathing suits, cargo shorts, tank tops, sweatshirts, sunglasses, sneakers, flip-flops.

"Help you?" asked a young woman behind the counter.

Kai turned and realized it was the one with the short black hair and blue eyes he'd spoken to on the sidewalk a few days before. Only now, instead of wearing a hooded sweatshirt, she was wearing a tight pink, low-cut tank top, revealing a figure that was guaranteed to keep male surfers of all ages coming back for supplies.

"Oh, it's you." She flashed him that bright white smile. "Been out lately?"

"A bit. You?"

"Only when I can drag myself out of bed. Usually I wait till after work to surf, if it's not blown out." She leaned forward on the counter, giving Kai an opportunity to inspect the merchandise more closely. "You ever go out in the evening?"

"Not much," Kai said. "I'm usually working."

"Too bad," she said. "You should try it sometime."

"I will," Kai said. "So where do they hide the boards in this place?"

The girl smiled knowingly and pointed toward a doorway. A sign near the ceiling said THE BOARDROOM.

"Thanks." Kai started that way.

"Hey," the young woman said. "What's your name?"

"Kai."

"Nice to meet you, Kai. I'm Jade."

Kai gave her a little wave. "Catch you later."

"I hope so."

Kai went into the boardroom. Even here a third of the room was filled with skim boards, skate boards, bodyboards, knee boards, carve boards. Another third of the room was dedicated to wet suits, surf bags, and board socks. When it came to actual surfboards, they were stuck in the back where they took up only the remaining third of the space, as if they were the last thing anyone wanted to sell. Kai doubted there were more than thirty in all, about what a surf shop a quarter that size might normally stock.

Something else caught his eye. Against one wall was a glass trophy case. Inside was a variety of surf trophies, bowls, and plaques. Many of the larger ones looked old and were inscribed to

Elliot "Buzzy" Frank. But there was also a row of newer, smaller ones inscribed to Lucas Frank.

"Impressive, huh?" A stocky guy with short red hair and a matching goatee joined him. The guy was wearing a flowery blue Hawaiian shirt and a pair of tan cargo shorts. His arms and legs were covered with thick mats of reddish hair.

"Yeah," Kai answered.

"At one time Buzzy was about the best there was," the guy said. "You know he's the owner of this store, right?"

Kai nodded.

"Now his son, Lucas, is coming up," the guy said. "Good strong young surfer. Anyway, can I help you with something?"

"Just looking," Kai replied, absentmindedly running his hand over a board.

"That's a nice one," the guy said.

Kai looked down at the board his hand had been on. It was some kind of machine-made composite thing, far too thick and wide for his tastes. "Nice for floating an elephant across a river."

The guy smirked. "That's a good one. Haven't heard it before. Just visiting?"

"I'll be in town for a while."

The guy offered his hand. "Dave McAllister. Chairman of the boardroom."

"Kai Herter."

"So, Kai, how just looking are you?" McAllister asked.

"Hard to say."

"What kind of board would you be interested in?"

"Guess it depends on what kind of waves you get around here," Kai said.

"Well, this is the northeast. Most of the summer you're lucky to get knee- to waist-high. Gets bigger in the fall, when the storms start blowing out of the tropics."

"I hear the waves get pretty good at that place called Screamers," Kai said.

"Uh, yeah, that's true." McAllister hesitated for a moment. "You'd be looking for something a bit shorter and more maneuverable then?"

Kai thought it was interesting that McAllister was so willing to sell him a board for a spot that "the chairman of the boardroom" assumed he'd never have a chance to surf. He let Dave show him a series of shorter boards that only a fairly experienced surfer would be able to ride. But Dave hadn't even bothered to ask Kai if he'd ever surfed before. The tour ended when a blond woman entered the room with a boy who looked around twelve years old. No doubt Dave saw a lot more potential for a sale.

"Take your time," he said to Kai. "Look around. Have any questions, you can always find me here."

"Thanks." Kai had seen enough. He was just about to go when he heard voices coming from the back of the boardroom. A door was ajar back there, and Kai caught a glimpse of a man sitting at a desk wearing an aqua blue polo shirt with SUN HAVEN SURF stitched in bright red over the pocket. It was the man he'd seen surfing with Lucas Frank the week before, which meant he was almost certainly the former northeast surfing champ Buzzy Frank. A couple of men in dark suits were sitting across the desk from him.

"Look, we hired you guys to find a way to get him out," Buzzy Frank was saying angrily. "Not to come back here and tell us all the reasons why you can't do it."

"I'm sorry, Mr. Frank, but there are limits to what we can do," one of the suits replied apologetically. "The man more or less abides by town ordinances. We tried to call attention to certain zoning violations, but he went and got those ACLU lawyers to show that he was being unjustly singled out. And just between you and me, Mr. Frank, he *was* being unjustly singled out and was entirely within his legal rights to do what he did. Laws have to be enforced uniformly."

"Or maybe we just need to hire some other, more imaginative, lawyers," Buzzy Frank said, in what was a not very subtle threat.

"You can go right ahead and do that," said the second suit, "but it sounds to me like what you really want is a couple of big guys with baseball bats and a can of gasoline."

"Come on, there's got to be something you guys can come up with," Buzzy Frank said, clearly frustrated.

"Honestly, Mr. Frank, if I were you, I'd stop giving money to lawyers and instead try to raise enough to make him an offer he can't refuse," said the second suit.

"You don't think we tried that?" Buzzy Frank replied. "We offered that fool two, three times what his property is worth, but he won't take it. Keeps chanting some nonsense about how 'it's not about the money . . . it's the principle.' The man's a drunk. He's irrational."

"You can't take a person's property away because he drinks too much," the first suit said.

"Why can't you just leave him there?" the second suit asked.

"Because it's a blemish on this community," Buzzy Frank said. "Do you have any idea how hard we've worked to turn this town into a premiere resort destination? Did you happen to see a McDonald's when you drove through? No, and you never will. Want to know why? Because fast-food joints cheapen the look of an area. We've spent hundreds of thousands of dollars keeping those kinds of places out. The only way we can grow this town into a first-class resort and increase real estate values is by bringing in high-end retailers like Banana Republic and Abercrombie. But every time a representative for one of those chains comes down the road and sees that rundown flop house of a motel they turn right around and go back where they came from. You think they're going to put one of their stores in a town with an eyesore like that? Not in a million years. And frankly, just between you and me, I think the son of a bitch knows that, and it's part of the reason he enjoys sticking it to us so bad."

"Well, Mr. Frank, I'm afraid we've done all we can for you," the second suit said. "As far as we can tell, we've exhausted every possible avenue. Other than buying him off the property, we can think of no other legal way of removing him."

Buzzy Frank stood up, but did not offer to shake the other mens' hands. "All right, that's it, thanks for nothing, gentlemen."

Kai stepped behind a rack of boards and watched the men in the suits pass. From inside the office came rapid beeps as fingers punched out a phone number. Kai peeked in through the doorway again. Buzzy Frank was still standing behind his desk, now pressing a small black phone to his ear. "Eric? Yeah, it's me. Yeah, I just had those jerks from Lipman and Kennelly in here. Total waste of time and money. Nope, nothing. At least, not legally. Yeah, damn right I told them to go to hell. What next? I've got some ideas. No, nothing I want to share just yet. What? Hell, no. This is far from over. Believe me, one way or another, that son of a bitch is going down."

Outside in the boardroom, Kai ran his finger down the slick, glassed deck of a bright yellow Channel Islands thruster. He was certain, almost beyond doubt, that the son of a bitch Buzzy Frank was so hot and bothered about was none other than Curtis.

Twelve

The swell was smaller the next morning. Only knee to waist high. It was still dark when Kai left the store. He planned to be surfing Screamers before the first local showed up, and to surf the entire day. It was one of those rare days when, for no apparent reason, his father told him to take off and not come back to the store until after dinner.

To Kai's surprise, someone got to the beach before him. In the dim predawn light, it took him a moment to make out the tall, thin figure and the long board lying on the sand. It was Bean.

"I knew it," Bean said when he saw Kai coming down the beach.

"How's that?" Kai asked, putting his board down and starting to wax it. The sky was lightening, now allowing only the brightest of stars to shine through.

"Don't know," Bean said. "I just knew it, is all. You don't seem like the kind who'd back down."

Kai finished waxing and picked up his board. "You coming?"

"Me?" Bean's brow furrowed.

Kai pointed toward Screamers. The waves weren't curling top to bottom the way they had the day before, but they were still breaking smoothly right to left. "Nobody's even out there yet."

"But you know they're gonna come," Bean said.

"Is it that bad here?" Kai asked. "You can't even surf a spot when no one's around?"

Bean stared down at the sand for a moment, then looked back up. "Okay, you're on. Let's go."

A few moments later they were both in the water, paddling toward Screamers. They hardly had time to catch their breaths when a waist-high set came in. Kai spun his board around and got on the second wave in the set.

He could see why Screamers was the primo break. The wave was faster and less sectiony. In no time he had five toes over the nose and was crouching back, feeling the board plane along the face. After he finished his ride, he saw Bean dropping off his board twenty yards away. The guy must have caught the wave after his. With a big smile on his face Bean raised his hand in a triumphant fist and pumped it. They both started to paddle back out.

"That was bitchin'!" Bean said once they were both outside again, sitting on their boards and scanning the horizon for the next set.

"Yeah." Kai felt himself smile. He'd already had a ride so good that the rest of the day would be icing on the cake.

"Can't believe I never rode here before," Bean said.

Kai didn't say anything, but he couldn't believe it either. As far as he knew, Bean had grown up here in Sun Haven. How was it possible he'd never surfed Screamers before?

"Uh-oh," Bean blurted out and gestured toward the beach. Three guys with short boards under their arms were giving Kai and Bean some serious stink-eye. One was Lucas Frank. The other two were also regulars at

Screamers. One was a big, muscular guy with a practically shaved head and a black barbwire tattoo around his neck. His surfing technique reminded Kai of a bullfighter intent on hacking every bull into pieces. The other was a slight black guy with dreadlocks, whose style of surfing showed some finesse and creativity.

The three short boarders hit the water and started paddling toward Kai and Bean, who immediately got prone on his board.

"Sorry, dude, this is where discretion becomes the better part of valor," he said, and started to paddle away toward Sewers.

A set came through, but Kai didn't take a wave. He preferred to wait and see what the locals did. Lucas and his brahs got out there and didn't even look at him. They just sat on their boards waiting for a wave, acting as if he wasn't there.

Kai saw another set coming and paddled to get into position. Being on the long board meant he could start farther out than the other guys. Out of the corner of his eye he saw the other guys paddling too. The set came in. Kai let the first wave pass. So did the other guys. The second wave was definitely rideable. Kai let it go. If the short boarders were there to surf, one of them would take it. But all three of them let it go. Now Kai understood what was happening. The third wave of the set was coming. Kai made no effort to take it. Then at the last second, he spun his board around and paddled hard, just managing to catch the wave. A second later the black guy dropped in on him. Kai had expected that, and as the guy dropped down the face of the wave, Kai put his weight on the toeside rail, forcing his board up and over the other surfer.

The black guy did a nice sweeping bottom turn and headed back up the face. Kai squatted and drove the nose of the long board down, picking up speed and outrunning the short boarder, who hit the lip and wheeled around. Once again Kai forced the long board up into the wave, but it was no longer a contest. The wave was losing its energy and there was no way the black guy could possibly catch him.

Kai dropped down on his board, turned it around, and began to paddle over the fourth wave of the set.

And that was when the big guy hit him.

Thirteen

Kai saw him at the very last second and ducked under the surface to avoid getting sliced apart by the guy's fins. He had no doubt the big guy had run straight over his board. When Kai came back up, the big guy was twenty feet away, already paddling out for the next wave as if nothing had happened. Their eyes met.

"Next time watch where you're going," the big guy said.

Kai started to swim toward him. The big guy stopped paddling and sat up on his board with a scowl on his face. Kai kept swimming. When he was three feet away, he dove. The big guy's legs were hanging down from either side of his board. Still under the water, Kai grabbed an ankle and pulled.

The big guy splashed into the water. Kai popped to the surface and waited. As soon as the guy's head came up, Kai swung.

The problem with fighting in the water was that there was no way to get any kind of power behind your punch. After all, you were floating without any footing and you more or less tended to just bounce off each other like human balloons. Kai's fist hit the big guy's head with about as much force as a wet towel. While it definitely caught him by surprise, Kai knew it probably hurt his knuckles more than the guy's head.

The big guy reacted by lunging forward with his arms spread like a lineman trying to make a tackle. Kai leaned backward in the water, brought his knees in tight under his chin and kicked out. The bottoms of his feet hit the big guy in the chest, but instead of knocking the guy away, Kai felt himself shoot backward in the water as if he'd just launched off the wall of a pool doing the backstroke.

Kai popped up in the water again. The big guy was about six feet away, splashing toward him with about as much grace as a gorilla in a ballet troupe. Kai was about to launch his next attack when he felt a neoprene-covered arm slide around his neck from behind.

The next thing he knew, someone had him in a sleeper hold, dunking him underwater, both choking and drowning him at the same time. His first reaction was to struggle, but he instantly realized that this would only use up the air in his lungs faster. So he went limp, and waited.

Whoever was choking him let him rise to the surface. Kai gasped for breath, but still didn't try to fight. With his head in that sleeper hold, he was being choked from behind. Any attempt to struggle would be insane. If the guy tightened his arm around Kai's neck, he could be unconscious in moments.

Meanwhile the big guy splashed toward him in the water, as if to hit Kai while he was being held.

"Back off, Sam," said the person holding Kai from behind. Process of elimination meant that this had to be Lucas Frank, since the black guy was still in the waves a couple of dozen yards away.

The big guy named Sam stopped in the water and glared at Kai, his teeth clenched and seawater dripping down his face.

Kai twisted his head around as far as Lucas would allow. "Think you could let go?"

"That depends," Lucas Frank said in the water behind him, keeping the hold around Kai's neck just tight enough to let Kai know he wasn't going anywhere until Lucas let him.

"Depends on what?" Kai said.

"On whether you agree to stay off our break."

"You own it?" Kai asked.

"Yeah," said Lucas Frank.

"What about the rest of the ocean? You own that, too?"

"Naw, you can have the rest of it," Lucas said.

With Lucas behind him, Kai couldn't see his expression. But he saw Sam start to grin.

"So?" Lucas said.

"So . . . what?"

"You gonna stay off our break?"

"No," Kai said, and felt the grip around his neck tighten.

The grin left Sam's face. He made a fist with his right hand. "Want me to smash him?" he asked Lucas.

"You ever have fair fights?" Kai asked. "Or you just like to hit people while they're being held?"

Sam's face darkened. "Let him go, Lucas."

Instead Lucas kept the hold around Kai's neck.

"Come on, Lucas," Kai said. "Why don't you let me go?"

"Shut up," Lucas snarled.

"Afraid I'll whip both your butts?" Kai taunted him.

"You don't fricken get it, do you?" Lucas said.

"I get it just fine," Kai answered. He was beginning to feel light-headed, the artery in his neck throbbing against Lucas's arm as it tried to deliver blood to his brain. "But I'll tell you what. If you're not going to let me go, would you at least ease up so I don't go unconscious and drown?" He felt Lucas loosen his grip just enough to allow the blood to flow.

"Stay off our break," Lucas said.

"It's not your break and I'll surf it anytime I want," Kai said. "And unless you're willing to kill me right now, you might as well get used to that."

Kai couldn't see the expression on Lucas's face, but Sam frowned and actually looked a little bewildered.

"I don't know what you think you're gonna surf on, tough guy," Lucas said, "because it looks like your board's in pretty bad shape."

Lucas turned Kai around so he could see the long board, floating about fifteen feet away with a six-inch gash in the rail thanks to Sam's fin. Realizing that it just as easily could have been a six-inch gouge in his head, Kai felt himself tense with anger. At the same time, Lucas took his arm from Kai's neck and shoved him away in the water. Kai turned and they came face to face.

"That could have been my head," he said.

"Maybe next time," Lucas said.

"Don't come back," said Sam, doing his best Vin Diesel imitation.

Kai forced his anger down. He'd be back as soon as he could. He turned and swam toward his damaged board.

Fourteen

"You know how close you came to being seriously maimed?" Bean asked on the beach when Kai came in. "I can't believe Sam did that. He could've killed you. And then you going after him like that. Dude, that was sick bold. What did Lucas say anyway?"

"Nothing intelligent," Kai said. Now that he was on the beach, he took a closer look at the gash in the board. It looked like someone had taken a saw to it. Kai winced. It was a serious bad ding and it wasn't even his board.

"Sam's got the brains of a tree stump," Bean said. "He's like Lucas's enforcer. You probably couldn't see how they did it. The only reason Everett, the guy with the dreads, dropped in on you like that was to distract you. So you wouldn't see Sam coming on the next wave."

"Yeah, now I know." Kai tucked Curtis's long board under his arm.

"What're you gonna do?" Bean asked.

"Get it fixed," Kai answered, and started up the beach.

Bean quickly picked up his board and joined him. "You're gonna have to take that to Teddy over on Third Street. I'll show you."

"Just tell me how to get there," Kai said. "You don't have to come with me."

"Oh, yes, I do," Bean said.

They got to the parking lot, went down a block, and turned left. Some early-morning tourists stared at them. Kai guessed it wasn't every day that people saw two guys in wet suits with boards under their arms, walking along the sidewalk through town. Especially when one was a guy with a long droopy mustache and thick black braid that reached halfway down his back.

"So what are you gonna do?" Bean asked.

"About what?"

"Lucas and Screamers."

"That's a nice spot," Kai said. "The wave has punch."

"Well, sure," Bean said. "I mean, why do you think those guys want to keep it to themselves?"

"Doesn't that bother you?" Kai asked.

"Sure it does," Bean said. "But what can you do about it? There's always three or four of them there, and you just saw what happens when someone tries to break into the lineup."

"We'll just have to see," Kai said.

They turned another corner, onto a block of residential houses. Bean stopped in front of a pink beach house with white shutters and a tall white picket fence. The fence seemed unusually high to Kai, as if its purpose was to keep a high-leaping animal in, or human beings out. Bean stretched up on his toes, reached over the gate, and opened the latch from the inside. There was no outside latch.

They went in, past flower beds filled with red and yellow rose bushes. The pink house was in perfect condition. The windows sparkled in the early-morning sunlight and inside each window was a white curtain. The flower boxes on the windowsills were filled with purple-and-yellow pansies. On the porch some wind chimes tinkled. Next to a single padded outside chair stood a small table with a book and a flower vase on it. It seemed to Kai that whoever lived there wasn't expecting company. All in all, the place didn't look like any ding-repair shop he had ever seen before.

"Around here," Bean said, leading him to the back of the house, where there was a large blue shed. Like the house, the shed was surrounded by carefully tended beds of flowers. A driveway paved with loose white pebbles led from the shed's garage-type door to a large white gate that prevented anyone on the street from coming in. Clearly this was the home of someone who demanded privacy.

As they circled around to the shed's side door, Kai heard jazz playing and the high pitched whine of a power planer mowing foam.

"Just let me do the talking." Bean laid his board down carefully on the lawn and knocked on the door. Inside, the power planer stopped. A moment later a small woman wearing goggles and a dust mask opened the door. Her brown hair was hardly longer than crewcut length and stood straight up on her head. She was covered with so much white foam dust that at first Kai thought she was a kid. She slid the mask and goggles off, causing a flurry of foam to flutter down around her. She glanced briefly at Bean and Kai and then reached for Kai's board, which he'd stood tail down on the grass.

"Where'd you get this?" she asked, scanning it from top to bottom. The board was nearly twice her height. She ran her fingers over some of the ding repairs and frowned with disapproval.

"Uh, Teddy, meet Kai," Bean said.

As if she hadn't heard him, Teddy turned the board around. Her eye stopped at the deep gash in the rail. She shook her head in disgust, as if she didn't have to be told how it happened. "What's wrong with those stupid kids?"

"Kai's new around here," Bean went on, as if he and Teddy were having two separate conversations.

"You know I don't deal with the public," Teddy said.

"Yeah, but Kai's cool."

"So's Frosty the Snowman."

Kai felt himself start to smile. Already he was starting to like her.

"Something funny?" Teddy asked.

"I like your attitude," Kai said.

Teddy's eyes hardened. "Go to hell. Flattery

will get you nowhere." She looked at the board again. "How in the world did I ever shape a piece of crap like this?" She obviously didn't expect either of them to answer.

"You shaped this?" Kai asked.

Teddy spun the board around so that Kai could see the bottom. She pointed at the initials TL on the stringer. "Theodora Lombard. This was the forty-third board I ever sold. Where'd you say you got this?"

"I didn't," Kai said. "Guy named Curtis gave it to me."

Teddy's face went stony.

"He doesn't know," Bean quickly said. "He just happened to run into Curtis and Curtis gave him this board."

"That's two strikes against him," Teddy grumbled.

"He surfed Screamers this morning," Bean said. "With Lucas and Slammin' Sam and Everett right there in his face." He patted Kai on the shoulder. "But no way did my man back down."

It was hard to tell if Teddy was even listening. "Curtis have any more of these?" she asked Kai.

"I don't know," Kai said. "There were all

kinds of boards in that yard. I even found an old Trigger Brothers back there."

"Someday I'm gonna go over there and take every single one of my boards back from that bastard," Teddy muttered, then looked at the gash again. "Will you look at how this thing's been treated?"

"I thought you said this was a piece of crap," Kai said.

Teddy focused on him for a moment. "It may be crap, but it's my crap. Curtis Ames does not deserve it. And neither do you." She tucked the board under her arm and turned to go back into the shed as if Kai and Bean had simply returned something that had always been hers. Just then they heard a beeping sound and turned to see a long bright red van backing through the white gate and up the driveway. On the side of the van in large yellow letters, was SUN HAVEN SURF.

The van stopped and Dave McAllister, the chairman of the boardroom, got out. He went around to the back doors and opened them. Inside were racks filled with surfboards. McAllister began to pull them out and lay them on the lawn.

"What exactly do you think you're doing?" Teddy asked.

"Surf camp starts tomorrow and Buzzy needs these boards tuned," McAllister said.

Bean cupped his hand close to Kai's ear. "That's Dave McAllister. Works in the board-room at Sun Haven Surf."

Kai nodded. "Yeah, I met him yesterday."

Meanwhile Teddy put her hands on her hips. "I know I didn't hear you right, Dave. You mean, he wants them next week?"

"Sorry, Teddy," McAllister said. "He really needs them tomorrow."

Teddy walked over to one of the boards, picked it up, and threw it back into the van where it landed with a loud clunk. Kai couldn't help wincing as he imagined the board banging into other boards or the van's walls. He wasn't sure what he was more impressed by—Teddy's strength or her guts.

"You tell that SOB Buzzy to take these boards and stick 'em where the sun don't shine," Teddy snapped. "What do you think I got here, a factory? There's just me, and I happen to have other things to do today."

Dave stared into the van, no doubt at the

board Teddy had just thrown in there. "Oh, uh, there's something I forgot to tell you, Teddy. Buzzy says he's workin' on an order for three new custom jobs. All long boards. Should be a real nice chunk of change for you and him."

Dave reached into the van and pulled out the board Teddy had just thrown in. He placed it on the grass with the others. In the meantime it appeared that the promise of multiple custom jobs had drained the fury out of Teddy. She crossed her foam-covered arms in front of her and fumed silently while Dave pulled the rest of the boards out of the van. As far as Kai could tell, all of them had minor crunchers, sinkers, nose or tail dings, rail fractures, etc. Nothing that would be too difficult to repair.

"You tell Buzzy I'll do my best," Teddy finally said. "But I'm not promising any miracles."

"I'll let you know about those custom jobs," Dave said, then got into the van and pulled out of the driveway. Kai, Bean, and Teddy were left inhaling a small cloud of exhaust.

"Okay, you two, help me get these boards into the shed," Teddy said.

The next thing Kai knew, he was helping Bean carry the boards into Teddy's shed. Like other shapers' shops Kai had been in, Teddy's was divided into two rooms—the smaller shaping room where she ground foam blanks into boards, and a larger room filled with blanks, rolls of fiberglass, cans of resin, half-finished boards on carpenter's horses, and shaped boards waiting for glassing.

If there was anything unusual about Teddy's shop, it was a lot neater and more organized than most, and had yellow curtains on the windows, a touch no other shaper— all the others Kai had known were male— had ever bothered with. Kai was also impressed by the number of boards and variety of shapes—from long to short and almost everything in between. Teddy was clearly a skilled and accomplished craftswoman.

As Kai and Bean carried the last board in and placed it on an upright rack, Teddy brushed the foam dust off her shoulders and walked up and down the line of dinged and bruised sticks. "Great, just freakin' great. Nine boards and he wants them all ready and dry by tomorrow morning."

"I could help you," Kai said.

Bean shot him a look and shook his head as if to say, "Keep your mouth shut."

If Teddy heard Kai, she didn't show it. Instead she picked up a board that had stress fractures running along most of one rail. It looked as if someone had dropped it on its side on the street. "Look at this." Teddy ran her hand along the damaged rail. "What do they use these things for? Batting practice?"

"I said I'd help you."

Next to him Bean rolled his eyes toward the ceiling, as if to say, "Heaven help us!"

Teddy turned and focused on Kai. "I heard you the first time, grommet." It sounded more like a warning.

Undeterred, Kai stepped over to a board with a cruncher in the rail, a spot where the fiberglass had been hit so that it was buried firmly into the foam beneath.

"What I'd do here is grind the area down, then build it up with layers of resin and cloth, then finish the job with a new coat of fiberglass."

For once Teddy actually seemed to be listening. "And what about this?" She pointed at a two-inch spot on the deck of the board, near the tail, where the fiberglass was separated from the foam underneath, a condition called delamination. Kai pressed his finger against the spot.

"Not worth fixing," he said. "It's delaminated, but it isn't cracked and won't let water in. These things are hard to fix and there's always a chance you'll wind up doing more damage."

Teddy's eyebrows rose. "Well, well, look at the brains on Mr. Grommet. If you know so goddamn much about ding repair, how come you don't fix your own freakin' ding?" She pointed at the ragged gap Sam had gouged in #43.

"Because I just moved here and I don't have the space or the materials yet," Kai replied.

Teddy stared at him, then at the boards, then back at Kai again. "Well, what are you standing around for? You gonna fix some dings or what?"

Kai looked down at himself. "All I've got is this wet suit."

"You live far from here?"

"No."

"Well, then go home and change, Mr. Grommet. Get your butt back here as soon as you can."

Fifteen

Kai and Bean left the shed. Outside, Bean picked up his board and they started down the sidewalk.

"She's a character," Kai said.

"No, she's not a character," said Bean. "She just plain hates everyone."

"How come?"

"I don't know the whole story. Just that she was a pretty hot surfer once. They started having contests around here and she wanted to compete, but there weren't any heats for girls so she wanted to go up against the guys, and somehow Curtis got involved and wouldn't let her. She's hated his guts and everybody else's ever since. Something like that. Most people say she's a wave short of a full set anyway."

"She doesn't seem to have a problem with you," Kai said.

"Yeah, well, I guess we outsiders have a common bond, you know? Besides, this is the second board I've bought from her, so she probably figures I'm a good source of revenue. I better warn you that she's pretty tight with a dollar. Before you do a lot of work for her you might want to make sure you're gonna get paid."

"Thanks for the advice," Kai said. They got to the corner. The boardwalk was one block to the right. The T-licious shop, one block to the left. "So you goin' back out?"

"Oh, yeah," Bean said. "Gotta get on it while you can, man. Summer's coming and it can get pretty flat out there."

"Catch you later," Kai said. "Have fun."

Bean turned toward the beach and Kai headed for the T-shirt shop. The sun was rising in the clear blue sky and the day was getting warmer. Wearing the wet suit, Kai was starting to feel like he was in a steam bath. He reached behind his back, pulled the zipper down and peeled the suit to his waist. That felt better. Instead of the hot and sticky wet suit, he felt his skin drying under the rays of the sun.

Two blond girls wearing skimpy shorts and bikini tops were coming down the sidewalk toward him, and as they got close, they started to stare and giggle. Kai casually ran a hand across his face to make sure there weren't any foreign objects hanging off his nose or anything. The girls passed, but when Kai glanced back over his shoulder, he saw that they'd stopped on the sidewalk behind him and were still looking and whispering. Kai was beginning to wonder if there wasn't something in the Sun Haven drinking water that made girls act strange.

He crossed the parking lot behind the T-shirt shop and let himself in the back door. Pat was in the back room staring at the computer. As soon as Kai came in, his father sat up straight and quickly hit some keys. "What are you doing here?"

"Just came back to change my clothes," Kai said.

"I told you to take the day off," Pat whispered hoarsely.

"I am," Kai said. "I'll be out of here in no time. What's going on?"

"Nothing," Pat said. "Don't go in the front. Just change your clothes and get the hell out of here and don't come back till dinner."

Kai rolled his eyes and started to pull off the wet suit. The Alien Frog Beast sat at the computer, impatiently rapping his fingertips against the desk top. Kai pulled on shorts and a T-shirt.

"See ya later," he said.

Pat ignored him. Kai headed out the back door of the shop, but he was curious now and went around the corner.

Out on the sidewalk in front of the store was a sign that read BATHING SUIT AND T-SHIRT MODEL AUDITIONS TODAY.

Kai could only shake his head in amused disgust. Pat and Sean really were a couple of dirt bags. It looked like they'd finally gotten the hidden cameras in the changing rooms to work. Those guys were sick puppies.

Kai walked to Teddy's, let himself through the tall white gate, and knocked on the shed door. When Teddy answered, she was covered with a new layer of foam crumbs and dust. It looked pretty obvious that she was more intent on shaping than ding repair that day.

"Ready to work?" she asked.

"Sure," Kai said as he stepped into the shop. "Any idea how you want to pay me?"

"That'll depend on the quality of the work," Teddy said. "Let's see how you do and then decide."

From living with Pat, Kai had become sensitive to all sorts of scams and cons. He could picture himself slaving over the boards for her all day just to hear at the end that she wasn't satisfied with the "quality" of his work. It was oddly similar to the "models" Pat would be "auditioning" and secretly filming in the changing rooms all day. There was no way Pat would ever actually hire a model.

But just because Pat was a con artist didn't mean Teddy was also. Kai's mom had taught him to always give people a chance before he judged them. He pointed at #43, the board Curtis had given him. "It's okay if I work on this one first?"

"Fine with me. Just make sure you get to the others so they'll all be ready by the morning. And go easy on the supplies, okay? I expect to find most of the fiberglass and resin on the boards, not on the floor."

"Gotcha."

"And if the phone rings, answer it and then bring it over to me," she said. "I don't always hear it in the shaping room."

Kai got to work. Whatever he knew about ding repair he'd learned from Ethan, his mom's boyfriend until she died. Ethan and his mom had lived together the last five years of her life, from the time Kai was eight until he was thirteen. Ethan was a freelance photographer from Chicago who'd been sent to Kauai by *Time* magazine and never left. He'd learned to surf and went out almost every day, did freelance work for surfing and travel magazines, and treated Kai like his own son. But Kai's mom and he weren't married, and after she died, things changed. End of story.

Teddy spent most of the day in the shaping room. The phone rang half a dozen times, and each time Kai answered it, brought the phone to Teddy, then went back to work. Of course, working so close together, he couldn't help but overhear her phone conversations. All of the calls were from people who either wanted to order a board, or had ordered a board and wanted to know when it would be ready.

Teddy treated them all with the same fine measure of disrespect. "If you want the board by the weekend, then why do you keep calling me? I can't shape and talk on the phone at the same time." She hung up.

"You think that's too much money? You can get a board from another shaper for two hundred dollars less? Well, good for you." She hung up.

"Why should I give you a discount for two boards? You think it takes me any less time to make two boards for one person than two boards for two people?" She hung up and glared at Kai. "Lord, what is wrong with these people?" By now Kai knew she didn't expect a reply. Instead she walked over to a ding repair he'd just completed and ran her finger over it. Then, without a word, she went into the shaping room.

Kai spent the morning and afternoon working on the dinged boards. Finally it was time to go. He knocked on the door of the shaping room. Teddy came out, covered, as always, with foam dust. "What?"

"Gotta go," Kai said.

Teddy stepped past him and inspected the repairs Kai had done. She checked the boards carefully to make sure he hadn't missed any dings either.

"Not bad," she said. "Come back tomorrow."

"Uh, I can't," Kai said. "I try to surf every

morning and then I usually work for my dad the rest of the day and night. I mean, we get flat conditions or it's blown out, I'll definitely come by."

"You gonna try to break into the Screamers lineup again?" Teddy asked.

Kai nodded.

Teddy smiled. "Then I'll probably see you here sooner than you think."

Sixteen

Back at T-licious the model audition sign had been taken in, but the other signs were still in the windows. Like SALE, 3 FOR $10 and SPECIAL THIS WEEK ONLY. All were offers designed to lure shoppers inside, where there was one small rack of really crappy T-shirts offered at three for ten dollars, and another marked SALE with equally crummy stuff. Most of the T-shirts on the shelves and racks had no prices at all. Instead they were sorted by names like Snow White Crew, Baby Blue V, and Daddy Long Sleeves. The same was true of the hundreds of colorful heat transfers hanging on the walls and displayed in glass cases. Instead of prices, they had serial numbers like 0LK793 or 32PU201.

The T-shirt names and heat transfer numbers meant nothing. They were part of the scam—creations of the Alien Frog Beast's warped and devious mind. When Kai entered the store around dinnertime, Sean and Pat were running a balls out con on a fancy-looking woman and her young daughter. The woman had seriously tweaked-out, dyed blond hair, industrial-strength perfume, expensive-looking clothes, and some major gold jewelry on her neck, wrists, and fingers. Her daughter, who looked like she was eleven or twelve, had multicolored braces, a cell phone snapped to her waist, and the permanent pout of a spoiled brat. For Pat this was a bonanza in the making.

The Alien Frog Beast sat by the cash register pretending to read a newspaper while Sean followed the mother and daughter around the store like a maid servant. There were other shoppers, almost all female, but Sean ignored them and focused on the mother and daughter. Sean's total attention to them must have seemed flattering, which was just what Pat wanted.

"Oh, Mommy, look at this!" the kid gushed, holding up a Pretty in Pink sleeveless tee.

The mother gave Sean a quizzical look.

Sean called over to Pat. "The Pretty in Pink, junior size two, sleeveless tee."

Pat put down the newspaper and pretended to thumb through a thick blue ring binder, as if looking for the price. "Eighteen ninety-five."

By now the daughter had moved over to the wall displaying the heat transfers. "Can I get one for the front and one for the back?" she asked Sean.

"Sure."

"Can I get three?" the girl asked.

"Yeah," Sean said. "You just want to keep it balanced, you know?"

"Then I could do four," the girl said, now in full design-your-own T-shirt creativity mode. "Two on the front and two on the back. That would balance, wouldn't it?"

"As long as it's tasteful," Sean advised like he was some kind of fashion consultant to the stars. Kai didn't know whether to laugh or barf. Sean wouldn't know what tasteful was if it came up and bit him in the butt.

It took a while, but the girl finally decided that she wanted her name, "Emily," spelled out in Day-Glo glitter letters (three dollars a letter) chest high with a glittery white unicorn (twelve dollars) underneath. On the back she wanted a glittery rainbow (nine dollars) over a glossy black galloping stallion (also nine dollars).

Sean took the Pretty in Pink T-shirt and heat transfers into the back room where the hot press was. Emily and her mom waited by the cash register. Pat went back to reading the newspaper. The minutes passed slowly. In the back Sean was probably glued to the computer, watching some girl try on T-shirts in the changing room. The delay was all part of the scam. Not only did you want to make it seem like a lot of work was involved in applying the heat transfers to the T-shirt (which actually took about a minute), but you wanted to make sure your customers were getting impatient and eager to move on to their next shopping experience. While Kai waited (Pat got royally pissed if you interrupted him during a con) he noticed a girl come in. She had light brown hair, freckles, and a cute smile, and looked familiar. Kai wondered if she'd been among the crowd of kids who'd come down to the beach the other morning when Bean and Booger thought Kai was going to challenge the local mutts at Screamers.

Emily's mom checked her gold watch and

tapped her foot. That was the sign Pat was waiting for. He put down the paper, swiveled around on his stool and called into the back. "How's it coming?"

"Pretty good," Sean replied. "Do they want color guard?"

Pat turned to Emily's mom. "Forgot to ask if you wanted color guard."

"What is it?" she asked.

"Ensures the colors don't run," Pat said. "It's only seven bucks."

Emily's mom nodded and Pat called back to Sean to do the color guard treatment. Kai had never seen a mother refuse color guard. After all, another seven dollars was definitely worth protecting all the other clothes in the laundry from being ruined by bleeding colors. Only there was no such thing as color guard. None of the heat transfers were made with water soluble ink that might run in the wash. It was just an easy excuse for charging seven dollars more.

Sean stayed in the back, still pretending to prepare the shirt. By now Emily had found a navy blue hooded sweatshirt she just had to have. Her mom said no and Emily started to whine. Emily's mom kept checking her watch and telling her daughter to shut up. She looked like she was going to scream if she didn't get out of there *right now*!

Finally Sean came out with the finished product and started to lay it out on the counter. "Would you like to see it?" he asked like it was a work of art he'd slaved over for years.

"Just put it in a bag," Emily's mom snapped.

Sean frowned in disappointment at her lack of appreciation for all the sweat and labor he'd expended. He put the pink T-shirt in the bag. Meanwhile, Pat added everything up on a calculator. The total came to seventy-six dollars and sixty-three cents with tax. (Pat, of course, never filed taxes so that just added to the profit.) Emily's mom practically threw her platinum card at Pat, who ran it through the machine. A few moments later she signed the receipt, grabbed her whiny daughter by the wrist, and stalked out of the store.

The bag with the T-shirt lay untouched and forgotten on the counter. Pat caught Kai's eye and jerked his head toward the door. Kai took the bag and headed out. Emily and her mom were on the sidewalk, both walking and talking on cell phones.

"I've had it with her," Emily's mom was

saying into her cell phone. "I'm bringing her home."

"My mom is so mean," Emily was saying into her cell phone.

"Uh, excuse me," Kai said behind them. Mother and daughter stopped and turned with phones still pressed to their ears. Both were frowning. They saw the bag in Kai's hand. Emily shrugged her shoulders as if she didn't even want it anymore. Her mother practically snatched the bag out of his hand. Kai figured the shirt would sit unworn in Emily's dresser for a few years and then get tossed.

He went back into the shop. Sean was now talking to the cute girl with the brown hair and freckles.

"How much is the Snow Man size large?" Sean called to Pat.

The price of every T-shirt depended on one thing only: what Kai's father thought the buyer could afford. "Fifteen ninety-five," Pat replied.

"What do you want on it?" Sean asked the girl.

"It's for my dad's fiftieth birthday," she said. "So I want it to say something like, 'World's Greatest Dad.'"

Kai could see the dollar signs light up in Sean's eyes. "No problem. What kind of letters?"

"Oh, I don't know. Maybe dark blue?" the girl said.

"On the front or back?"

"The front, I guess."

"You don't want to leave the back blank, do you?" Sean asked, as if leaving the back that way was considered really, really bad taste.

"I guess not," said the girl.

"What's he like to do?" Sean asked.

"Fish. That's what he loves best."

"Check some of these out." Sean led her over to a display case. Inside were all kinds of heat transfers of fish and fishermen. "You could even add something on the back like, 'A bad day of fishing is better than a good day at work.'"

"He'd love that," said the girl.

Sean and Pat would love it too, since all those letters pushed the price of the T-shirt into the stratosphere. Meanwhile the girl picked out a large heat transfer of a bluefish and striped bass leaping out of the water.

"Okay," Sean said, summarizing the sale. "'World's Greatest Dad' on the front. Bluefish and striped bass on the back with 'A bad day of fishing is better than a good day at work.'"

The girl nodded.

"Why don't you tell her what it'll cost," Kai said.

Sean froze and stared at Kai in disbelief. Over by the cash register, Pat's look was considerably more menacing. A big part of the con was to never state the price before the heat transfers went on. Once the heat transfers were done, customers rarely refused to pay, regardless of how outrageous the price was. After all, they'd created the unique custom shirt themselves and everyone understood that no one else would want to buy it.

"Why don't you go in the back," Pat grumbled.

Kai didn't move. The girl gave him a curious look. Pat continued to glare at him, then pretended to add up some figures on the calculator. "Looks like the total comes to thirty-nine ninety-five."

Kai estimated that Pat had just cut twenty dollars off the price he had planned to charge her, but the girl still looked surprised. Her eyes widened, then she frowned and looked down at the floor.

"She's probably not going to need the color guard," Kai said. "So you can take seven off that price. And if you use the soft felt letters instead of the glossy ones, she can save another three."

The soft felt letters were less expensive than the glossy ones, but they looked and felt a lot better on the shirt. Pat narrowed his eyes venomously and pretended to push more buttons on the calculator. "Guess that makes it twenty-nine ninety-five," he growled.

"Sounds right," Kai said. He took the shirt and heat transfers from Sean. "I'll do it."

He was in the back room laying the letters on the shirt when Pat came in and closed the door behind him. "I ought to—"

"What?" Kai said without looking up from the hot press.

"Beat the living crap out of you."

Kai just stood there and waited, as if inviting him to try.

"You want to play hero to the chicky-poos, that's your business," Pat growled. "Just not on my dollar, understand?"

Kai got the letters spaced evenly and pulled down the cover on the hot press.

"I don't need this shit," the Alien Frog Beast went on. "You want to be on my team, you play by my rules."

Team? Kai thought. If this was a team, he'd

do anything to get traded. He lifted the hot press cover, turned the shirt over, and started to lay out the letters on the other side.

But Pat wasn't finished. "Let's get one thing straight, sonny boy. I didn't want you, got it? When she was pregnant I told her to get rid of it, but she went ahead and had you anyway. It was her decision, not mine. I don't even know why the hell I bother to keep you around, but you pull another stunt like that and I'll cut you loose so fast you won't know what hit you. Got it?"

Kai finished laying out the letters on the back and pulled the lid of the hot press down again.

"Now, you get your act together, hear me?" Pat said. "Or the next time this boat leaves port you won't be on board."

"Is that a promise?" Kai asked, and lifted the hot press lid. He felt the heat on his face and picked up the warm T-shirt. "Excuse me." He brushed past his father and headed toward the front of the store.

The girl was waiting by the counter. Kai folded the shirt and put it in a plastic bag and handed it to her.

"Thanks." She flashed him a big smile,

then lowered her voice to add, "And thanks for helping me save some money."

Sean was over on the other side of the store already working on the next marks—a pair of blondes wearing shorts and bikini tops. Kai realized that they were the same two he'd passed on the sidewalk earlier in the day, and that right now they were spending more time looking at him than at the T-shirts Sean was trying to sell them. Meanwhile Pat was still in the back. Kai leaned over the counter toward the girl with the cute smile and freckles. "Listen," he whispered, "next time you want to buy a custom T-shirt, try one of the other stores in town."

The girl frowned.

"Trust me," Kai said.

Seventeen

At sunrise the next morning, Kai was on the beach again. The swell had gradually dropped for the past few days, and today it was mostly knee high with a rare waist-high set mixed in. The slight onshore breeze at that early hour was a bad sign. If it got any stronger it would quickly blow out such weak surf.

For now, Kai didn't care. He was just happy to get out, especially early in the morning, when he could be alone. He waxed the board, went in, and paddled out toward Screamers. The water was particularly clear this morning, and Kai could see the sandy bottom. Out over the horizon the red-orange sun was just starting to come up. Paddling through the troughs between waves, Kai looked up and could see the outline of the sun through the thinning crests rising before him. It reminded him of Hanalei, only there it was the opposite: The only time he'd seen the sun through the waves was at sunset, not sunrise.

No sooner was he out at Screamers than a set came in. Kai caught the second wave with a single stroke of his arms, popped up and rode the board down the line. It felt great to glide along the curl, but a little bit frustrating, too. He'd begun to get his surf legs back and starting to miss having a short board. Turning the old long board was like being the "steer man" in the back of a *waa,* one of those big Hawaiian outriggers they used as a tourist attraction. Once in a while he could manage a clumsy snap or off-the-lip on old #43, but floaters, aerials, cutbacks, and all the other moves he loved were completely out of the question.

As the wave lost power, Kai kicked out and started to paddle back. He wasn't surprised to see two more surfers paddling out: Lucas and Buzzy Frank. Both saw him, and Kai couldn't tell who looked more surprised, the son or the father. Then Lucas gave his father a shrug, as if to say, "Don't worry about him. I'll deal with it later."

They got outside. Kai, being on the long board, went out farther than Lucas and his father. Even though that meant that Kai could have gotten on the waves sooner than Lucas, each time a set came in, he let Lucas take a wave first. It wasn't that he was afraid the guy would try to run him down from behind the way Slammin' Sam had the day before. Instead it was Kai's way of acknowledging that he was an outsider and showing that he actually believed in the concept of wave sharing. That it was okay to let a good wave go by so that someone else could have a shot at it instead of having to catch every curl within reach. At the same time, once Lucas was on a wave, nothing was going to stop Kai from taking the one after it.

After letting Lucas choose the waves a few times, Kai caught Buzzy Frank giving him a funny look, as if he knew what Kai was doing, but couldn't understand why.

Meanwhile the waves weren't the only things being ridden hard. Buzzy Frank was working his son over big-time. "The only way you're gonna throw spray today is by taking off later and deeper in the pocket. The place you're taking off, you might as well be on a goddamn long board."

"Dad, the waves are only knee high," Lucas complained. "What difference does it make?"

"Plenty," Buzzy Frank shot back. "You think I'm gonna call off a contest on a day like today just because surfers aren't happy with the conditions? This is what contests are about. It's about making something happen in slop. Any grem can tear it up in head-high conditions with an offshore breeze. It's the guys that can do it in crap, sectiony waves like this, that make it to the pros."

Then, as if he'd planned it all along, Buzzy Frank caught what had to be the wave of the day—a nearly chest-high freak that seemed to jack up straight out of nowhere, pulling the water before it tight and smooth and breaking left. Kai and Lucas both watched as Buzzy took off down the face, did a sharp bottom turn, headed back up and smashed the lip, sending a fan of spray high into the air. From there he somehow almost managed to get tubed and finished with a floater before dropping down into the soup.

Even in Hawaii Kai hadn't seen many guys that age surf that well. Clearly at some point in Buzzy's life he indeed must have been a top surfer. Meanwhile Lucas shook his head bitterly, as if he couldn't believe that particular wave had come along just at the perfect time for his father to show him how it was done.

"Don't waste water," Buzzy told his son as he paddled back out. "Use every inch of it. And remember. No matter what they say, more spray equals more points."

Kai looked down at the deck of #43 and scratched at a lump of wax with his fingernail. He was only fifteen and already he had seen enough of that hypercompetitive ego vibe to last a lifetime. There was nothing wrong with anyone who wanted to surf in competitions. The problem was when that whole competitive vibe spilled over into average days and local breaks where people just wanted to enjoy themselves.

Twenty minutes later the onshore breeze suddenly kicked up a notch, more or less blowing out what was left of the surf and making it look like a washing machine. Lucas and his father caught waves in. Kai stayed out a little longer, hoping for one last good ride.

By now white caps were starting to appear and the surf was getting lumpy and irregular. Waves popped up out of nowhere as if by magic, then disappeared just as quickly. Finally Kai realized it was hopeless and rode the soup in.

Once again Kai passed Buzzy and Lucas in the parking lot while they stripped out of their wet suits beside the big yellow Hummer. This time Lucas leaned toward his father and whispered something Kai couldn't hear. Buzzy lifted his head and gave Kai a quizzical look. Kai nodded back. Buzzy blinked and looked away.

Real friendly types, Kai couldn't help thinking.

In the parking lot behind T-licious, Kai hosed himself, the board, and wet suit off with a garden hose attached to a spigot on the wall. He left the board and wet suit to dry in the sun and went in the back door with his towel wrapped around his waist. It was still about an hour before opening time and neither Sean nor Pat were there. Kai assumed they were having breakfast at the diner. He was about to go into the bathroom to finish drying off when he happened to glance out into the store. Something pink was taped to the outside of the glass front door. It looked like a small envelope.

Kai pulled on a pair of jeans and a T-shirt, then unlocked the front door and took in the envelope. It smelled like perfume, but had no address. Kai tore it open. Inside was a party invitation for that Friday night. Someone had written a note on the bottom in red ink.

> *Hi,*
> *I'm the girl who got the shirt for her dad's birthday yesterday. I don't know your name, but I hope you will come to my party.*
>
> *Shauna*
>
> *P.S. It's okay if you want to bring some friends.*

Eighteen

A little after 10 P.M. on Friday night, Kai met Bean and Booger under a streetlight on the corner near Sun Haven Surf. Bean was on foot. Booger had come on a carve board. A strong breeze from the south made the flag in front of the bank across the street flap noisily. The wind had been steady for three days straight, blowing out the weak surf. Kai had spent his early mornings in Teddy's workshop, where she was now letting him do some of the preliminary board work like scraping crust and sanding some of the Clark foam blanks before she did the fine tuning on the rockers, rails, and hulls.

"How come we had to wait so late to go to this party?" Booger asked.

"I had stuff to do," Kai answered.

"What kind of stuff?" asked Bean.

"I work till ten most nights," Kai said.

"Where?" Booger asked.

"It doesn't matter," Kai said. "Anyone know where Livingston Street is?"

"It's a couple of blocks from where I live," Booger said. "Up the hill behind St. John's Church. How old is this girl again?"

"I don't know," Kai said. "I guess about our age."

"What'd you say her name was?" Booger asked.

"Shauna."

"You ever hear of anyone named Shauna around here?" Booger asked Bean.

Bean shook his head.

"I just don't want to be the youngest one there, you know?" Booger said. "Cause then the older guys like to show off to the girls by picking on you, and the girls treat you like you're their little brother."

"How do they treat you if you're the old-est?" Bean asked.

"Like you're weird," Booger said. "But with you they'd be right."

Bean took a half-serious swing at Booger,

who dropped his carve board to the street and quickly skated out of range.

Across the street a car slowed down. The driver stared at them. She was blond, and the car she was driving was a red Thunderbird. The tan convertible top was up. There was someone in the passenger seat, but that person was in the shadows and Kai couldn't see.

"Deb Hollister," Bean said. "Lucas Frank's girlfriend. That's gotta be Lucas in the car with her."

"What's the driving age around here?" Kai asked.

"Seventeen," Booger said.

"She's eighteen," Bean said. "Just graduated with me."

"How old's Lucas?" Kai asked.

"Fifteen or sixteen, I think," Bean said.

Across the street the red Thunderbird sped up and disappeared around a corner.

"Nice car," Kai said.

"Her dad owns the local dealership," Bean said.

"Maybe I'll just go home," said Booger.

"Why?" Kai asked.

"It's all gonna be older kids," Booger said. "I just know it."

"Let's see, okay?" Kai said.

They started to walk uphill, away from the shoreline. Kai noticed a strange scent in the air. It was cologne, coming from Booger. The houses they passed were smaller than the summer places near the beach. They looked more like year-round residences. Kai had the feeling that most of them belonged to people who'd lived and worked in Sun Haven for most of their lives.

A car cruised past with three girls in it. Kai was starting to get the feeling that a lot of kids around Sun Haven had vehicles.

"You got wheels, Bean?" he asked.

"Uh, yeah. I'm having some work done," Bean said. "Should be ready in a few days."

"Know what Bean's dad does?" Booger asked as he skated beside them. "He's an undertaker."

"That so?" Kai said.

"Family business," Bean said.

"Bean's gonna be an undertaker too," said Booger. "He's going to undertaker university in the fall."

"New Canaan College of Mortuary Science," Bean corrected him. "It's a one-year program."

"Then we can call him Doctor Death," said Booger.

"No, Boogs, I'd have to get a PhD to be called that."

"Tell Kai about the ones that drown."

"Grow up, Boogs," Bean said patiently.

"First they sink," Booger said, "but then they start to decompose and they fill up with gas like a balloon and float to the surface."

"Hey, Boogs, you want to be a big hit with the girls tonight?" Bean asked.

"Uh, sure," Booger said eagerly.

"Then keep that stuff to yourself."

They got to Livingston Street and went left at the corner. A few houses ahead, some girls were sitting on the steps leading up to a porch.

"I'm glad this is near where I live because if everyone's older than me I'm just going home," Booger said nervously.

As they got closer Kai recognized Shauna, the girl with the freckles, sitting with two girls, who both had dark hair and looked like sisters. The younger sister was drinking a diet Coke, the older, a Coors Light. Kai turned up the walk and stopped at the bottom of the steps.

Shauna smiled. "Hi."

"Hey," said Kai.

"I was starting to wonder if you'd make it," she said.

"I hope it's okay that I brought some friends," Kai said.

"It's great," Shauna said, gesturing to the two girls with dark hair.

"So where's the party?" Booger asked.

"This is it," Shauna said. "I'm new here. These are my cousins, Sara and Pauline. They're visiting for a couple of days."

"This is Bean and Booger," Kai said.

Sara, with the diet Coke, and Pauline, with the Coors, giggled.

"Those aren't your real names, right?" Pauline asked.

"They call me Booger because I'm a spongehead," Booger said.

"What?" asked Sara.

"I body board," Booger explained.

"What's your real name?" Pauline asked Bean.

"Lawrence."

"Why do they call you Bean?" she asked.

"I don't know," Bean said. "But it's been so long since anyone called me by my real name, I'm not sure I'd know who they were talking about."

"What's your name?" Shauna asked Kai.

"Kai."

"That's different," said Pauline.

"It means ocean in Hawaiian," Kai explained.

"Are you from Hawaii?" Sara asked.

"Well, sort of," Kai said. "My mom moved there when I was really young and we stayed until about two years ago."

"Then what happened?" Pauline asked.

"I moved back," Kai said.

"What about your mom?" asked Shauna.

Kai shrugged. He didn't feel like announcing it to everyone. A silence followed. Kai looked up at the stars. He suddenly became aware of crickets chirping and the sound of TV coming through an open window from the house next door. Out of the corner of his eye he thought he saw Shauna arch an eyebrow in Pauline's direction.

"So what's that?" Pauline pointed at Booger's board.

"A carve board," Booger said.

"Like a skateboard, right?" said Sara.

"No, way better. You want to see how it works?"

"Sure." Sara got up and went down the

steps behind Bean and Booger. Her older sister, Pauline, glanced in Shauna's direction again.

"Aren't you going to check it out too?" Shauna asked.

Pauline rolled her eyes in a way that made Kai think she wasn't thrilled about getting paired with Bean. "Why not?" she said, mixing the words with an unmistakable sigh. She got up and went down the steps. Shauna's house was on the hill and under the streetlight Booger started to show Sara how the carve board worked. Bean and Pauline stood several feet apart and watched.

Kai sat down near Shauna on the steps. "Thanks for inviting me."

"Thanks for coming," Shauna said. "And thanks for helping me in the store the other day. What's with that place?"

"It's a scam," Kai said.

"Why do you work there?" she asked.

"It's a long story," Kai said. "You got a beer or something?"

"Oh, gosh, I should have offered. Coors Light okay?"

"Sure."

Shauna went into the house and came out with a beer for Kai and one for herself.

Kai took a cold slug. "So did I see you in that crowd down at the beach the other morning?"

Shauna nodded.

"How'd you hear about it?" Kai asked.

"You know the ice-cream shop on the corner of Main Street and Second Avenue?" Shauna said. "I work there and all these kids were coming in and talking about how there was going to be this big showdown at the beach the next morning, so I went. How come you left?"

"I wasn't there to entertain everyone," Kai said. "I was there to make a point. Only with that crowd it was going to be a lot harder to make."

"What point?" Shauna asked.

"That no one has the right to decide who can or can't surf a break," Kai said. "Waves should be free for whoever wants them."

"That's why all those guys were waiting out there on their surfboards?" Shauna asked.

"Yeah. They're all locals and they think they own that break, and they were out there to make sure no one except them surfed it."

"Aren't there lots of other places to surf around here?" Shauna asked.

"Yes, but that's the best place."

A laugh drew their attention to the street. Sara was trying to stand on the carve board. Her sister Pauline was holding one of her arms and Booger was holding the other.

"So what happens now?" Shauna asked. "I mean, about the point you wanted to make?"

"I went back the next morning," Kai said. "When no one was around."

"And?"

"I made my point."

Shauna gave him a puzzled look. "What happened?"

"I guess you could say we had a run-in. My board got pretty badly dinged."

"And are they going to let you surf their break?" Shauna asked.

"It's an ongoing thing," Kai said. "Might take a while, but sooner or later I think they'll get the idea."

"You must really like to surf if it means that much to you," Shauna said.

Kai nodded.

"Did you learn in Hawaii?" she asked.

"Yeah. My mom started me when I was little. I was so small I couldn't even paddle into the waves so she used to have to push me. She said by the age of five I was starting to rip. Where're you from?"

"Connecticut. My dad was a commercial lobsterman up there, but the lobsters in Long Island Sound died off."

"How come?" Kai asked.

"Nobody really knows. Some scientists think it was because of all the chemicals people put on their lawns. Anyway, we moved here because my dad got a job as a trawler captain."

"Was there any surfing in Connecticut?" Kai asked.

Instead of answering, Shauna grinned.

"What's so funny?" Kai asked.

"All you think about is surfing," she teased. "Anyway, no, there wasn't much in Connecticut, but some kids went up to Rhode Island."

"You ever go?" Kai asked.

Shauna shook her head. "Maybe you'll teach me."

"You need a board," Kai said.

"I've got one," Shauna said. "Or at least, there's one in the basement. I guess the people who used to live here left it when they moved."

"Serious?" Kai was instantly curious about any board, intentionally left behind or not.

"I don't know if it's any good," Shauna said. "I mean, it looks really big to me. You want to see it?"

"Sure."

Shauna got up and Kai followed her into the house and down some stairs that led to the basement. Like the basements of most homes near the ocean, this one felt damp and smelled sour like mildew. Shauna turned on a light. The basement was filled with commercial fishing gear—basketball-size spools of 120-pound clear monofilament line, nets, blue-and-yellow nylon ropes, bright red plastic floats. In the back, under a few spider webs, leaning lengthwise on the floor against a wall was one of the largest surfboards Kai had ever seen. It had to be at least eleven feet long, five inches thick and nearly two and a half feet wide at its widest point. From the color and condition of the yellowed, delaminating fiber-glass, and the almost semicircular, fixed single fin, Kai could tell that it was probably thirty or forty years old. He couldn't get over the size of the thing. As if it had been shaped for the Incredible Hulk.

"No surprise the previous owners left it," Kai said as he ran his fingers over the dusty rail. "They probably couldn't figure out how to get it out of here."

"It's no good?" Shauna asked.

"Not really. Way too big and too old," Kai said, lifting the tail. The thing weighed a ton. Too heavy, too, he thought, looking around the basement. How in the world did they get it down there?

"So I can't use it?" Shauna sounded disappointed.

Kai looked at the old board again. Big boards were sometimes called tankers because they reminded people of oil tankers. This thing qualified as a supertanker. He looked back at Shauna. Her shoulders had dipped and she was pursing her lips. Not just disappointed, she was seriously bummed.

"Hey," he said. "You want to learn to surf that bad, you can use my board."

"Really?" Shauna's eyes widened and she stood taller and grinned. "You mean it?"

"Yeah, sure."

"Would you show me how?"

Kai hesitated. He didn't mind letting her try old #43, but the last thing he wanted was to get roped into a bunch of lessons.

"We should probably go back up before the others start to wonder," Shauna said, biting her lip and giving him a strange look as if maybe she wished something *would* happen to make them wonder.

"Right." Suddenly feeling claustrophobic, Kai headed for the stairs. Behind him Shauna was no longer smiling.

Nineteen

Back outside, Pauline was now trying to ride the carve board. Bean was trotting beside her, one hand around her waist and the other supporting her arm, the way people did when they were trying to help their friends learn to ice skate. The carve board was picking up speed and Bean had to run to keep up. His long black braid bounced against his back.

"Don't let go!" Pauline screamed with a laugh.

Meanwhile Booger and Sara were sitting on the curb under the streetlight talking. Booger was smoking a cigarette. The kid was trying too hard to be cool.

"Looks like your friends are hitting it off

with my cousins," Shauna said, a bit wistfully. "Want another beer?"

"Sure. Thanks."

Shauna went inside and came back with two more cold ones. She and Kai sat down on the steps again.

"So what about your mom?" Shauna asked.

Kai took a deep breath and let it out slowly. "She died. In a car accident."

"Oh, I'm sorry, Kai." Shauna sounded like she meant it.

"You see, there are these really narrow bridges on the north shore of Kauai," he started to say. "And—"

"Kai?" Shauna interrupted.

"Yeah?"

"You don't have to tell me."

It was strange, but Kai hadn't realized what he was doing. He was telling her, and he'd never told anyone before. Of course, a lot of people on Kauai knew the story from the papers or their friends. But he'd never told a soul on the mainland. He'd never even talked to his father about it. The truth was, he wasn't even sure if Pat knew how his mom had died.

"I want to," Kai said.

"Then you should."

"So they have these really narrow bridges. If a car is going across one, any car going in the other direction is supposed to stop and wait because there's no way two cars can pass at the same time."

"Someone didn't wait?"

Kai nodded.

"God, Kai, that's awful."

It was worse than awful, but Kai hadn't told her the whole story.

A car came down the street. It was practically in front of Shauna's house before Kai realized that it was Deb Hollister's red Thunderbird. The top was down and Lucas was sitting in front with Deb. In the back were Sam, Everett, and a red-haired kid with a shark's tooth hanging around his neck who Kai had seen in the Screamers lineup. The car stopped by the curb and all four guys got out. Lucas's girlfriend got out and leaned against the door with her arms crossed. Lucas and his crew stopped at the bottom of the steps.

"We heard there was a party," Sam said.

"What do you want?" Kai replied.

"Now, is that being friendly?" Lucas asked.

"About as friendly as you guys are out at Screamers," Kai said.

"Listen, dickhead, you want to surf Screamers you got to earn the right," Sam said.

"Says who?" asked Kai.

"Me," Sam said. "You want to do something about it? Or is this another one of those times when you're gonna run away?"

"Well, I'll tell you, Sam. You just gave me no choice." Kai started to get up. Sam might have stood a few inches taller and weighed fifty pounds more than he did, but if the big slob wanted a piece of Kai, he was going to get his chance right now.

"Wait a minute." Shauna jumped up and stood between them. Kai was impressed, considering she was smaller than either of them. "If you want to fight, go do it someplace else."

Kai and Sam glared at each other over Shauna's head.

"I'd like you to leave," Shauna said to Sam and the others from Lucas's crew. She held up a small silver cell phone. "Right now or I call the police."

Lucas's posse looked to him for a sign of what to do next.

"We were going anyway," Lucas said. "This scene sure isn't happening." He turned to Kai. "Tell you what. You want to be in the Screamers lineup so bad? When the next good swell comes in, why don't you have a heat against Sam? You win, you can surf Screamers anytime you want."

"Me *and* my friends *and* anyone else who wants to surf there," Kai countered. "If I win, Screamers is open to everyone."

"Aw, that's fricken bogus," said the kid with the shark's tooth.

"Chill, Runt," Lucas said, and turned back to Kai. "What's the point of that? You let everyone in the world onto Screamers, it'll be a zoo out there. No one'll get a wave. And even if they do there'll be some bozo paddling out right into his path and he'll have to bail or run him over."

"I thought you guys liked running people over," Kai said, glancing at Sam.

"You deserved it," Sam growled.

"Shut up, Sam," Lucas said, then turned back to Kai. "I'm serious. The place would be a mob scene."

"If someone paddles into your wave you take 'em aside and explain that next time they should paddle around," Kai said. "As far as Screamers becoming a zoo, the rule still stands. The wave belongs to the first man up. It wouldn't stay mobbed for long. A lot of guys would get tired of missing waves and move over to Sewers or another break."

"Yeah, but a lot would stay, too," said Runt.

"Okay," Kai said, "so maybe you'd get three less rides a day than you usually get. Would that kill you?"

"Know what?" Lucas said. "It sounds great, but it's a load of crap and I'll tell you why. This is a tourist town and all summer long new yahoos show up with boards thinking they can rip anywhere they want. So it's not like it's a local group of guys who'll get the idea sooner or later. It's new kooks everyday paddling in the way, dropping in on your waves, and screwing everything up."

"Anarchy," Everett said softly.

"Whatever you want to call it," Lucas said. "I go out there to surf, not be some fricken surf cop."

Kai shrugged.

"Okay, listen," Lucas said. "Here's a compromise. You win the heat, you and your friends can surf Screamers. But not the whole world."

Kai didn't answer. He was thinking.

"Who's gonna judge this heat?" asked Booger.

"We'll each bring two judges," Lucas said. "That way it'll be even. What do you say?"

Kai said nothing. He disliked surfing competitions and what they'd done to the sport. He also knew that unless Lucas and his posse wanted to kill him or break his legs, there was no way they could keep him off Screamers forever. But that wasn't the point either. The point was that Screamers should have been open to everyone. But the only way guys like Bean and Booger would ever get on those waves was if he agreed to compete.

"I'll think about it," Kai said.

Lucas made a big show of letting his arms flop to his sides, as if to say he'd tried his best but Kai was being totally unreasonable.

Of course, Sam read Kai's answer a different way. "What's this? Do I smell tuna? As in chicken of the sea?"

Kai made a fist and stepped toward him. Suddenly they were bathed in flashing red and blue lights as a green-and-white Sun Haven patrol car pulled up in front of the house. A police officer got out and put on his hat. "All right, let's break it up."

He pulled out his flashlight and shined it around, pausing for a moment on the empty beer cans on the steps, then on their faces, stopping when he got to Lucas and Sam. "Hey, Lucas, Sam."

"Hey, Officer McCann," Lucas said in a way that clearly showed they knew each other.

"There a problem here?" McCann asked.

"Naw," Sam said. "We came for a party, but it turned out all they were serving was chicken of the sea." He and the others headed back toward the street and Deb Hollister's car.

Twenty

It was late and quiet. Even the crickets had grown silent. A quarter moon hung overhead and the sky glittered with stars. Bean and Kai walked down the dark empty street toward town. In front of them, Booger made long lazy arcs on the carve board, passing in and out of the streetlights.

"So what'd you think of those girls?" Booger said. "I think Sara really liked me."

"Oh, yeah?" Kai had more or less forgotten about that part of the evening.

"You think I should have asked for her phone number?" Booger asked.

"Sure, why not."

"Darn, you're right. I should have. Too late now."

"No, it's not. She's staying with Shauna," Kai said. "Just call Shauna's house."

"You know Shauna's last name?" Booger asked.

Kai shook his head.

"Well, that's that," Booger said, as if it was hopeless.

"Then just go over there tomorrow," Bean said. "You know where she lives."

Booger bit his lip. "You'll come with me, right?"

"You don't need me," said Bean.

"Aw, come on, I can't go alone," Booger said. "How about you, Kai? Don't you want to see Shauna? Anyone can see she really likes you."

"I can't go tomorrow," Kai said. "I have to work in the afternoon and there's other things I have to do in the morning."

"Work at Teddy's?" Bean asked.

"No, something else."

"Then what about the day after?" Booger asked.

"Seriously, Booger, just go down to the beach tomorrow and hang out," Kai said. "You know Sara and Pauline are gonna show up there sooner or later. I mean, what else do people do around here on a sunny day?"

"Well, I'll think about it," said Booger.

They kept walking. The loudest sounds were their footsteps and the squish of the carve board's rubber tires.

"So, was the reason you didn't agree to a heat with Sam because you're pretty much a long boarder and there's no way a long board can compete with a short board?" Bean asked Kai.

"I'm actually much more of a short boarder," Kai said. "I just don't have one."

"Then, uh, how come you didn't agree to the heat?" Booger asked as he rolled past them in the dark.

"Because for me personally, surfing competitions are bogus," Kai said. "I mean, everybody has their own reason to surf and I respect that. If Sam and Lucas want to compete, that's fine for them, but I don't happen to agree with it."

"Why not?" Bean asked.

"Because the way I feel, surfing is about riding," Kai said. "Not trying to jam as many tricks and as much spray as I can into one wave. If I feel like doing an off-the-lip, great. I want to do a backside rail grab, cool. But to me it's because it's fun. It's part of the ride, and if I'm on a wave, and just cruising feels right,

I don't want to force something that doesn't belong there."

"But you could if you wanted to, right?" Booger asked. "I mean, you've got all the moves, don't you?"

It was a good question, Kai thought. He'd definitely had them once, but that was a long time ago.

"You should do it, man," Booger said as he glided into a circle of light on the carve board. "Even if it's just once. It would be so sweet to see Sam get his lunch served to him. And then I could finally get tubed at Screamers and retire."

"Retire from what? You're fourteen years old," Bean said.

"I don't know, it just sounded good," Booger said.

Bean and Kai shared a smile. They got to a corner. Bugs and moths fluttered and zipped insanely around a streetlight.

Booger hung a big wide carve onto the next street. "Later, dudes. I'm going this way. Bean, I'll see you in the morning if it ain't blown out."

Kai and Bean waved good-bye and kept walking downhill. The town of Sun Haven had gone mostly dark by this hour. Beyond the orderly rows of streetlights and the thin dull ribbon of beach, the Atlantic Ocean spread out like a vast black oil slick.

"Kook," Bean said in a low voice.

"Who? Booger?"

"Yeah."

"He's just a kid," Kai said.

"Dude, he's only one year younger than you," Bean said.

It was true, and Kai could only assume that the difference between him and Booger was that he'd seen and been through a lot more crap in his life than most guys his age.

"Think there'll be any surf in the morning?" Bean asked.

Kai could feel the cool ocean breeze in his face. "That onshore wind is still blowing."

"Yeah, what a pain," Bean said.

They kept walking.

"I don't know about Booger and Sara," Kai said, "but it looked like you and Pauline got along pretty good. You get her number?"

Bean pulled a small flip phone out of his pocket. "Already memorized. So what's this thing you have to do tomorrow morning?"

"Just personal business stuff," Kai said.

"Like?"

Kai gave him a helpless look.

"Hey, sorry," Bean said. "It must be private or you would have told me. Right?"

Kai raised a shoulder and let it drop.

"You know, Kai, I don't know you very well," Bean said, "but there's one thing I do know for sure. You may be fifteen, but you're carrying some kind of heavy load."

Amen, Kai thought.

Twenty-one

The next morning Kai walked down to the beach wearing a pair of jeans and a sweatshirt. The sky was a vast blanket of light gray clouds and the combination of weak swell and onshore wind made the surf look like spilled beer—all foam and not much else. A trawler moved slowly out on the horizon with a small white cloud of terns and seagulls following in the air behind it. Kai wondered if it was Shauna's father's boat.

Kai glanced over at Screamers. Even there it was a lost cause—the waves coming off the jetty were flopping over into mushburgers. But suppose it was a perfect day, Kai thought. Suppose Lucas and his crew were out there, keeping everyone else out of the lineup. Suppose, just suppose, he did surf against Sam. He'd need a short board.

Kai got to the beach and walked along the water's edge. The sun was hidden behind the clouds and the sand was cool under his feet. The steady onshore breeze felt damp and smelled like seaweed. A dead brown horseshoe crab lay on its back at the waterline. Kai knew that if he was back on Kauai he would have asked Ethan, his mom's boyfriend, what he thought. Ethan was good with these kinds of things. He had a different way of looking at life and sometimes came up with angles Kai hadn't thought of. But Kai wasn't on Kauai, and Ethan was just a memory.

When the red roof of the Driftwood became visible over the tops of the dunes, Kai turned up the path that led to the motel's backyard. If he couldn't ask Ethan, he wondered if he could talk the deal over with Curtis and see what he thought.

When Kai came through the bushes, he found a strange scene. Curtis was sitting in one of his rusty beach chairs, staring at something. The older man glanced briefly at Kai with watery, bloodshot eyes, then looked away without nodding or saying hello. Kai stopped. Something was wrong. Curtis was staring at the shed where he kept his good boards. Kai noticed that one of the shed's doors was hanging open at a slant, as if the top hinge had pulled loose.

Kai took a few steps. He could see into the shed. The wet suits were still hanging against the back wall, but the surfboard racks were empty. Now he understood what the busted door meant. Someone had broken into the shed, probably with a pry bar from the looks of the splintered wood where the lock had been forced.

Kai glanced around the yard, as if hoping Curtis's prized sticks might be there, scattered among the dozens of other boards.

"They're gone," Curtis said.

From ten feet away, Kai could smell the liquor on the man's breath. An empty Jack Daniels bottle lay on its side on the ground near the chair.

"When?" Kai asked.

"Last night as far as I can tell."

Kai felt his shoulders slump. It was a mad crappy world where someone stole someone else's surfboard. "Any idea who did it?"

"Plenty," Curtis replied, but didn't elaborate.

"Want some coffee?" Kai asked.

Curtis shrugged, but Kai had a feeling he wouldn't refuse it once it was in his hands. Leaving Curtis in the chair in the backyard, he walked around to the front of the motel and in the door marked OFFICE. Inside, he went around the counter and through the door that led to Curtis's apartment. He found himself in the living room. The place was a wreck, the coffee table piled high with surf magazines, empty liquor bottles, and plates with the dried-out crusty remains of half-finished meals. The air felt stale and smelled slightly of garbage. Kai had a feeling it had been a long time since a window had been opened. The floor in front of the TV was littered with surfing videos and DVDs. The walls were covered with pictures of waves and epic breaks and that famous old pink-and-orange *Endless Summer* poster with the round yellow sun and black silhouettes of surfers carrying long boards on their heads. In the bottom right corner was an inscription in black Magic Marker:

To Curtis,
Great surfing G-Land with you.
Looking forward to our next trip.
Hang ten, man.

Bruce

In the surfing world there was only one G-Land. It was a place of perfect waves off the island of Java in Indonesia, halfway around the globe. Kai studied the note closely. Bruce could only be Bruce Brown, the man who'd made the most famous surf movie of all time, *Endless Summer*, and its sequel, *Endless Summer II*, and whose son Dana had made the awesome *Step into Liquid*. It was amazing to think that Curtis actually knew, and had surfed with, people like that.

Kai went into the kitchen, which was in even worse condition than the living room. It stank from rotting garbage. The sink was filled with dirty glasses and dishes. Some were partly covered by fuzzy greenish mold. Kai didn't want to think about how long those dishes had been there. The coffee pot was half filled with cold coffee. Kai emptied it over the dirty dishes hoping the coffee might kill some of the mold. The glass in the coffee pot was brown with residue, the kind of thing that could only happen if you didn't wash the pot for years.

Kai started to search for a new coffee filter. That's when he noticed that against the backsplash beneath the kitchen cabinets were framed photos of a much younger Curtis with dark hair and a tanned, streamlined build. Always wearing surfing trunks, usually with a long board propped beside him. In one photo he was standing with Greg Noll, otherwise known as Da Bull. Noll was a legend in the surfing world, believed to have ridden the largest wave ever seen at Makaha. There were photos of Curtis with other surfers Kai didn't recognize, but he suspected they too were among the famous founding fathers of West Coast surfing. And then there was a photo of Curtis with a short, shapely brown-haired young woman in a red bathing suit, both of them holding boards, and Curtis's arm around her waist in a manner that suggested they were more than just friends. Kai looked away, then thought of something and looked back at the photo again. The young woman was Teddy.

Kai finally found the coffee filters and got

a pot going. While he waited, he figured he might as well clean up a little and opened the cabinet under the sink to look for a garbage bag. He found some, but there was also a large moldy old cardboard box under there. Curious, Kai opened it. Inside were two dozen rusted surfing trophies, a bunch of silver awards bowls tarnished so brown you could no longer read the inscriptions, and plaques screwed to wood that had gone spongy and rotten from years under the leaky sink. Kai closed the box, kept the garbage bag and dumped the kitchen garbage into it, more than happy to tie the bag closed and seal off the stink.

A little while later Kai carried two mugs of coffee out to the backyard. Curtis hadn't budged. He was still sitting in the old beach chair staring into the empty shed. Kai handed him a mug, then sat down cross-legged on the damp, dew-covered grass.

Curtis took a sip. "Thanks, grom."

"There's a bunch of trophies in a box under the sink," Kai said.

"Yeah, well, I guess there was a time in my life when I thought that stuff was important."

Kai waited for him to continue. When Curtis didn't, he said, "And?"

"And then one day I realized trophies are like hemorrhoids. Sooner or later every asshole gets one."

They both sipped coffee and stared at the empty shed. It was hard to imagine why anyone would do such a terrible thing. Kai could see how some strung-out junky or desperate soul might steal one board and sell it just to get some fast cash. It was harder to imagine some dirtball surfer taking a board, but also possible, although, if the dirtball surfed anywhere around Sun Haven he risked getting nailed. But to take all of a man's best boards? That was as low as you could go.

"You think maybe it was someone staying here?" Kai asked.

Curtis shook his head. "I considered it, but then I thought about who'd been here this weekend. All regulars, and not one with any kind of vehicle capable of hauling that many boards. I had some ten footers in there."

They sat quietly. Now and then a thin flicker of yellow sunlight managed to squeeze through the cloud cover, but it remained chilly and gray. After a while Curtis said, "Thing like this makes me wonder if it ain't about time to go."

"Me?" Kai asked, thinking Curtis meant he wanted to be alone.

"No, grom, not you. I meant me. Time to get away from here. And away from all this crap."

"Where would you go?"

"Don't exactly know. Someplace where I'm wanted, that's for sure. Or at least, someplace where people don't give a hoot one way or the other and are willin' to leave a man alone."

"You leave and there won't be any place left for surfers to stay around here," Kai said.

Curtis smirked. "Welcome to the real world, grom. You think the city fathers don't know that? It's all economics. What do you think the average surfer who stays in my place spends in this town? Twenty-five bucks a day on food, surf wax, and beer? Hell, they tear my place down and build some fancy resort or condos or some such monstrosity and they'll have tourists staying here who spend more than twenty-five bucks just on breakfast each morning."

"Has anyone ever offered to buy this place from you?" Kai asked.

"Of course," Curtis answered with a bitter

laugh. "About once a week, grom. And for good money, too. Enough so I could buy a condo in Oahu and never work another day in my life."

Kai didn't have to ask the next question. It was obvious.

"You want to know why I never bailed?" Curtis said. "I'll tell ya. Because I can't stand what's happening in this country. Goddamn coastline's gettin' out of reach to everyone who ain't rich. You talk to anyone who's been surfing for more than twenty years and they'll all tell you the same thing. Up and down the coasts. West coast. East coast. Gulf coast. From Florida to New Hampshire, Pensacola to Galveston, and San Diego to Oregon everyone can probably name a dozen great breaks they once could surf but they can't get close to now. Why? Because it means crossing private property, or breakin' some lame local town restriction, or payin' prohibitive parking fees. I've held on to this place all these years because I can't stand seeing the rich bastards win. I wanted a place where anyone could come and surf his nuts off. Or *her* nuts off. And believe me, grom, they tried to get me out any number of ways. When they couldn't buy me out they assigned a cop to this place to ticket everything possible. Littering, jaywalking, public consumption of alcohol, illegal parking. I finally had to get an ACLU lawyer to go to court charging that I was being unfairly singled out. Then they tried to pass a bunch of stupid ordinances to harass me out. Why, they even passed one limiting the number of surfboards you could have in your yard. Can you imagine that? Had to get the ACLU for that one, too. But this"—he nodded at the empty shed— "this is the lowest thing they have ever done."

"You sound like you know who did it," Kai said.

Curtis shook his head. "At this point I could name two dozen individuals, maybe more, who might have done it. When you stand up for what you believe in, you make a lot of enemies, grom."

Kai thought of Lucas and his crew.

"But it almost don't matter this time," Curtis went on. "Even if it wasn't someone from this town . . . just some stranger, it still depresses the hell out of me. The idea that someone would walk onto a man's property and take, not one or two of his best boards, but every single damn one of them." Curtis swept his arm around gesturing at the dozens and dozens of old boards piled up around the yard. "Hell, they could have taken twenty, thirty of these pieces of junk and I wouldn't have cared. But to take my best boards . . . the ones I treasured most."

Curtis stared down at the ground. He took a sip of coffee and winced, then held the mug out to Kai. "Do me a favor, grom. Top this here off with a healthy blast of JD, okay? You'll find a fresh bottle in the cabinet over the sink."

Kai carried the coffee mug back around to the front of the motel and went into the kitchen. There were half a dozen new bottles of Jack Daniels in the cabinet over the sink. Kai opened one and did as he was asked, then went out to the backyard again.

"Thanks, grom." Curtis took a gulp and shivered. "Top o' the morning to ya."

"You can't let 'em win," Kai said.

Curtis held up a wavering, weather-beaten hand to stop him. "Save it, grom. I've been fighting this battle since before you were born two times over. I've fought long and hard enough to be able to do whatever I goddamn well please. S'cuse my French, but tryin' to break into the lineup at Screamers ain't doodly squat compared to the battles I've fought."

"You know about me and Screamers?" Kai asked, surprised.

"Grom, if it has to do with surfing and Sun Haven, I know about it."

"What do you think I should do?" Kai asked.

"Do about what?"

"The heat with Slammin' Sam."

"What heat with Slammin' Sam?"

"I thought you just said if it had to do with surfing and Sun Haven you knew about it," Kai said.

"For Christ's sake, grom, you see a fricken crystal ball here? I'm talking about the big issues, not every little intragrommet wave quibble. So let me guess, if you beat Sam in the heat they'll let you into the Screamers lineup, right?"

"Me and my friends and anyone else who wants to surf there."

"Whoooo. Big stakes." The sting of Curtis's acid sarcasm burned.

Kai got to his feet. "I'm truly sorry about your boards, Curtis. Honest. And I hope you don't let anyone chase you out of town. If there's any way I can help you, I will."

Curtis stared into the shed, almost as if he hadn't heard Kai.

"See ya." Kai started back down the path to the beach.

"Hey, grom," Curtis said.

"Yeah?" Kai stopped.

"You really want to help me?"

Kai nodded.

"Go find my fricken boards."

Twenty-two

Each day got a little hotter and sunnier. The winds died down, but so did the swell. Instead of a disorganized bowl of suds, the surface was now crystalline and flat. The beach was getting more and more crowded, and as a result, there were fewer shoppers in town during the day. People were starting to go into the water, but it was still around sixty-three degrees so they didn't stay in long. To keep store owners happy, and to give the shoppers a reason to shop, the town decided to have a sidewalk sale. Pat had Kai move the sale rack and the "3-for-$10" T-shirt rack out on the sidewalk and keep an eye on them in case there were any T-shirt thieves around. Kai sat in a beach chair in the shade with a notebook of lined paper on his lap and sketched the people who passed.

A red convertible Thunderbird pulled up to the curb and Kai found himself face-to-face with Deb Hollister. Sitting next to her was Lucas Frank. Sam and Everett were in the backseat.

"Still thinkin' about it?" Lucas asked.

Kai looked back down at his notebook and kept sketching.

Lucas looked at the T-shirt racks. "So this is where you work?"

Kai nodded.

"Your father run this place or something?"

"Yup."

"What happens in the winter?" asked Sam.

"It gets cold and sometimes it snows," Kai said.

Sam frowned, but Lucas grinned.

"Yeah, very funny," he said. "So what do you do then?"

Kai could have answered, "We wear coats," but there was no point in pushing the joke any further. "We usually head south."

Lucas tapped his fingers against the car door. "So you'd go through all this grief just to get into a lineup for two or three months?"

"I'm not trying to get into the lineup," Kai said. "I'm trying to make a point. That it's not fair for you guys to keep other surfers off Screamers."

"Yeah, yeah," Sam said. "We've heard that whole argument."

"So everywhere you go you try to break into every local lineup you can find?" Everett asked.

Kai shook his head. "It's been a long time since I lived anywhere near a break. Until we got here I hadn't seen an ocean for two years. After this summer it might be another two years until I see one again."

"Why can't you just relax and enjoy the summer instead of starting a fricken war?" Sam asked.

"People have a right to surf anyplace they want," Kai said.

"You open up Screamers to every crumb-snatcher who comes along with a piece of foam between his legs, you're not gonna get any waves either," Lucas said.

"Maybe not as many as some hard charger local," Kai said, "but I'd still get my share."

The guys in the car glanced at one another.

"You're crazy," Sam said.

"The place would be a zoo," said Lucas. "Waikiki Beach."

"The rule would still apply," Kai said. "The wave belongs to the first man up."

Lucas shook his head. "It'll never work."

"And it ain't gonna happen anyway," Sam said. "Because you're too chicken to surf, and even if you did, you'd get your butt waxed."

Kai knew Lucas was watching to see how he'd react. He leaned his chair against the wall, kept sketching and said nothing. Lucas turned to his girlfriend. "This is stupid. Let's go."

The car rolled away, every piece of chrome glinting under the hot sun.

"What was that about?" someone asked.

Kai looked to his right. Shauna was standing on the sidewalk about ten feet away, the hot sun beating down on her head. Unlike a lot of girls, who went around town wearing bikini tops, she wore a light blue T-shirt.

"Nothing," Kai said.

She stepped into the shade of the awning and looked down at the notebook. "You're an artist?"

"Not really." Kai closed the notebook. "I just like to draw sometimes."

"Bet you wish you were surfing right now."

"Sure. You know what they say. A bad day surfing is better than a good day at work."

"That's what it says on my dad's T-shirt about fishing."

"I thought your dad's work *was* fishing," Kai said.

"He still likes it." Shauna flashed her smile. "Did you go this morning?"

Kai shook his head. "It's been flat. Ankle slappers at best."

"What about tomorrow?"

"The forecast is to stay small at least till the weekend."

"Too small to teach?" Shauna asked.

"Probably just the right size to teach," Kai said.

Shauna raised an eyebrow slightly. Kai thought about it. Normally he would have gone to Teddy's to do ding repairs, but with hardly anyone out surfing in the ankle-high waves, Teddy had no work for him.

"You got a wet suit?"

"I'll borrow one."

"All right," Kai said. "Tomorrow morning. Sunrise."

Twenty-three

The next morning Kai sat on the beach and watched the waves roll in. They were small, but clean, and it would be a good day for a lesson, if Shauna showed up. Kai watched the little waves lap at the shore and the foamy water run up the sand and then back down. It reminded him of Hawaii. His mom always took him to the beach. He remembered seeing pictures of himself crawling at the water's edge in a diaper even before he had learned how to walk. Lord, he missed Hawaii. The memories filled him with mixed emotions. The yearning to go home, but also the painful recollections of what had happened there.

Kai heard the pad of bare feet on sand and

turned, expecting to see Shauna. Instead he found Lucas and his father coming down the beach. Lucas was wearing a shorty wet suit and carrying a board. Buzzy was dressed in his "business" clothes, khaki slacks and an aqua blue polo shirt with SUN HAVEN SURF stitched in bright red over the pocket. Kai couldn't imagine that either of them thought Lucas could ride a short board in surf so weak.

As father and son passed Kai, Lucas gave him the slightest nod. Kai returned it. At the end of the dry sand, Buzzy stopped and helped Lucas zip up his wet suit. Then Lucas took his board and splashed into the water.

Kai watched Lucas paddle out. Instead of stopping at the end of the jetty where he'd normally catch a wave, Lucas turned to the right and kept paddling parallel to the beach for about two hundred yards down to Sewers, then he turned in. He actually managed to briefly catch a small wave, but all he could do was hop it for a dozen yards. Then he finished paddling to the beach, got out of the water, tucked the board under his arm, sprinted back toward his father, and then headed in again.

Now Kai knew what was going on. Lucas

was doing endurance work. Specifically, practicing for competition in a strong rip or drift, where competitors were pulled far down the beach and then had to run back so that they'd be in front of the judges for their next ride. It seemed as if Buzzy Frank was a master at figuring out ways to take something that should have been fun and turn it into work.

"Sorry I'm late!" someone called out behind him. Kai turned and saw Shauna trotting over the sand toward him carrying a green-and-yellow towel and a black wet suit. "I had to help my dad load some fishing gear into his pickup."

"No problem," Kai said.

"Great, so what do we do?" Shauna asked.

"First you put on the wet suit," Kai said.

"Okay." Shauna pulled her light blue hooded sweatshirt over her head. Underneath she was wearing a red bikini. Kai noticed that while she wasn't built like the models in the *Sports Illustrated* swimsuit issue, her figure was almost perfectly proportioned. She picked up the wet suit and started to pull it on.

Kai had to smile. "Stop."

Shauna looked up, surprised. "Why?"

"The zipper goes in the back."

"Oh, sorry." She pulled off the wet suit and started again.

"Don't sweat it," Kai said. "Everyone does that the first time. It's the ones who do it the second time that you have to worry about."

Even before Shauna got the wet suit all the way on, Kai could see that it was way too big for her. "Where'd you get this thing anyway?"

"It used to be my brother's," she said. "I mean, when he was younger. It doesn't fit him anymore so I thought it would be okay if I borrowed it."

Kai didn't have the heart to tell her that it was too big to be much help. Once she had the wet suit on, he showed her how to lie on the board and then pop up into a standing position.

"The key is to go all the way up," he told her. "You don't want to get into the habit of going to your knees and then getting up. It's all one motion."

Shauna tried it. "How do I know which foot to put in front?"

"Good question." Kai stepped behind her and without warning gave her a slight shove. Shauna lurched forward and put out her right foot to stop herself.

She turned, looking surprised and hurt. "Why'd you do that?"

"That's how you tell," Kai said with a smile. "You're goofy."

"What?"

"You're goofy foot. When you push most people, they put out their left leg. They ride left leg forward, right leg back. When you're goofy, you do it the other way around."

"What do you do?"

"I'm what they call switch foot. I do it either way."

"Is that something you learn to do when you're good?" Shauna asked.

"Some people do," Kai said. "For me it just came naturally."

Shauna practiced popping up a few more times. Being small, light, and strong, she had no problem doing it.

Kai picked up #43. "Okay, you're ready. Let's go."

They waded out until the water was almost chest high. Kai held the board aimed toward shore while Shauna climbed on and lay down. "I'm going to wait for a wave and give you a little push to get you going, then you pop up," he said. "There's just a couple of other things. You don't want to ride the board all the way into shore."

"Why not?"

"Two reasons. The first is if you fall off the board in a few inches of water you can hurt yourself. The second is you can ding the nose and mess up the fins. So when you get close to the shore you want to jump off."

"Anything else?"

"Not really. With the waves this weak you're not going to have to worry about the board hitting you. If you can, try to fall off to the side."

"I can see why I wouldn't want to fall off in front of the board," Shauna said. "I could get hit. But why don't I want to fall off the back?"

"The way boards are designed, if you fall off the back, the tail sinks down and the whole board shoots forward. So if you're shallow, the fins could hit the bottom and the board could go flying onto the beach. And if you're ever surfing in a crowded spot and you let the board shoot out like that you could really hurt someone."

"But don't most boards have leashes?" Shauna asked.

"Yes, but if you had a nine-foot leash on

a nine-foot board you could hit someone almost twenty feet away. You want to learn to control the board yourself. Not use the leash to do it for you. And anyway, you don't have a leash."

"Anything else?" Shauna asked.

"Nope. That's it. Hold on."

A little wave came and Kai gave the board a push. As soon as she was moving, Shauna tried to pop up. She instantly did a header off the side. A moment later she stood up with her face covered by wet hair.

"You okay?" Kai asked.

Shauna nodded and pushed the hair out of her face. For some people it only took one fall to decide they preferred miniature golf. The board had drifted in toward the beach. Shauna got it, then came back out. Without a word, she turned it around so it faced the beach and lay back down.

The next wave came and Kai gave the board a push. Shauna popped up, immediately lost her balance and fell, this time banging her elbow against the deck as she went down. Kai winced. Shauna stood up, rubbed her elbow, pushed the hair out of her eyes, and went to get the surfboard.

On the third try Shauna actually managed to stand on the surfboard for a moment before toppling over. This time when she stood up in the water, she was smiling.

After a few more tries Shauna was able to pop up and stay up.

"Great," Kai said when she brought the board back out to him. "You're ready for the next step. This time you don't get on. Instead you stand next to the board and hold it while you wait for a wave. When you see it come, push the board forward and jump on like it was a sled. Then pop up and ride."

The first time Shauna tried it, she got on the board too far forward and immediately pearled and did a nose dive. The next time she overcompensated by getting on too far back. The little wave rolled under the board and left her floating behind.

"What am I doing wrong?" she asked.

"Nothing," Kai said. "Every board has a sweet spot. It's where you have to be to catch the wave. If you're too far forward, you'll pearl. If you're too far back, the board won't trim and you just stall."

"How do you figure out where the sweet spot is?" Shauna asked.

"By doing exactly what you're doing," Kai said.

Shauna kept practicing. Kai was getting cold, and since he no longer had to be in the water, he bodysurfed back to the beach and watched from there. He also watched Lucas continue to make his round trips, paddling out, then down to Sewers, then in, then running back up the beach. It seemed to go on for a lot longer than the typical twenty-minute heat. Buzzy obviously wanted his son to be in righteous shape.

"Hey," someone said.

Kai turned. It was Jade, the pretty young woman from the surf shop. She was wearing a heavy gray sweatshirt that hung down to her thighs. Her legs were bare underneath.

"Hey," Kai said.

"Giving someone a lesson?" She nodded toward Shauna, who was still out in the water.

"Yeah," Kai said.

"You always come here in the morning?"

"If it isn't blown out," Kai said. "What are you doing here so early? Thought you said you could never get out of bed."

"I can when there's no one else in it," Jade answered.

The words hung in the air between them.

"I'll keep that in mind," Kai said.

Jade smiled. "I wish you would. So how's the water?"

"Without a wet suit?" Kai said. "Definitely refreshing."

"Good. I feel like getting refreshed." Jade pulled the sweatshirt off. Underneath she was wearing a blue bikini. The bottom half fit perfectly around her shapely hips, but the top was a little too skimpy to fulfill its job requirements, especially when Jade dropped the sweatshirt to the sand and bounced into the water with a splash.

To be honest, Kai was surprised when Jade stood up and the bikini top was still on. Considering the force with which she'd dived into the water, it could easily have slid off. Now that she'd splashed into the icy water, the thin material left almost nothing to the imagination.

Jade was out of the water as fast as she'd gone in, jogging toward him. Kai had to work very, very hard not to stare.

"That was great," she gasped, pulling the sweatshirt back on.

"Looked like you enjoyed it," Kai said.

"Looked like *you* enjoyed it too," Jade replied with a knowing wink.

Kai felt his face turn red.

"Hey, don't be embarrassed," Jade said. "I like providing enjoyment." She touched the tip of his nose with her finger. "But only to certain people. See ya." She headed back up the beach. Kai couldn't help turning and watching her go. Some invitations were easy to pass up. That one wasn't.

"Did you see it?" Shauna asked.

Caught by surprise, Kai turned and found her standing beside #43 in the shallows. "Huh?"

"I did it! I caught a wave and popped up! Didn't you see it?"

Kai nodded.

Shauna pouted. "You're such a liar. You were watching her. Isn't she a little old for you?"

"Uh . . ."

"Oh, forget it." Shauna grinned. "I did it. I caught a wave and stood up! I really did!"

"Way to go." Kai was honestly happy for her. She was stoked.

"Yeah." Shauna's lips were blue and her teeth were chattering. Just as Kai had expected, the oversize wet suit was no protection from the cold water.

"What do you say you take a break and warm up?" Kai said.

"Okay."

She came up the beach and sat down next to him. Kai quickly saw that she was trembling uncontrollably.

"You'll warm up faster if you get out of this thing," Kai said, and helped her out of the wet suit.

Shauna toweled herself off and pulled on her sweatshirt. She was still shivering, but not as violently. "Kai, thank you for showing me. That was great!"

"I'm glad you like it," Kai said. Some of the beachcombers were out by now. The only other people around were Lucas and his father.

"That's him, right?" Shauna said.

Kai nodded.

"What's the hassle between you two?"

Kai explained the age-old problem of localism.

"What if you were a local?" Shauna asked. "Wouldn't you want to keep everyone off your break?"

Kai felt a knot in his heart. He had been a local once. A dumb gremmie who thought he was hot stuff. He'd done some really stupid things and learned a terrible lesson. "I sure hope not."

Shauna studied him closely, as if she saw the painful memory in his eyes. "What is it about surfing you love so much?"

"It's hard to put it into words," Kai said.

"Try? For me?"

"Well, I guess part of it is the amazing feeling of riding on water," he said. "I mean, sometimes it's almost like flying. And if you catch some air, it really is like flying. The other thing is, when you catch a wave, it gives you its energy. You harness it and control it. Sometimes I wonder if that's where the aloha spirit of giving comes from."

"What's that?"

"It's this thing the Hawaiians believe," Kai said. "If someone needs something you give them whatever you have."

"Like teaching them what you know?" Shauna asked.

"Yes. So you're on the wave. If you're in the pocket, you're almost in the wave. What's propelling you and the board forward is pure energy. To me, surfing is about sharing, controlling, and using that energy. You become one with the wave. All together it's this indescribable feeling of freedom and power and cleansing the soul."

"That's pretty good for someone who didn't think he could put it into words," Shauna said.

"That's me." Kai smiled. "The Shakespeare of surf."

They both grew quiet, watching Lucas run up the beach and hurl himself on his board out into the little waves. "Who's the other one?" Shauna asked.

"His father," Kai said. "Buzzy Frank. Former competitive surfer. Owns that big surf shop in town."

They watched Lucas paddle out. This time, instead of paddling parallel to the beach, he saw a wave and turned the board around to catch it. A moment later he was up.

"Why's Lucas bouncing up and down on the board like that?"

"It's called hopping," Kai explained. "Short boarders do it to keep momentum in crappy surf."

"If the surf is so crappy, why are they out there today?"

"Buzzy's trying to get him into shape. He's also trying to show him how to make the most out of so little."

"Why?"

"'Cause if you're gonna be a champion surfer, you gotta rip in all conditions," Kai said.

"Lucas wants to be a champion surfer?"

"I'm not so sure," Kai said.

"Do you want to be a champion surfer?" she asked.

Kai shook his head.

"Did you ever?"

Kai was quiet for a moment, then he said, "Yeah. There was a time when I thought it would be pretty cool to get paid to surf the best spots in the world."

"What changed?" Shauna asked.

Kai shook his head. He couldn't talk about it.

"You have lots of secrets," she said.

Kai stood and picked up #43. Then he walked down to the water and dipped it in to get the sand off. He came back up the beach with the board under his arm. Shauna joined him, carrying the wet suit wrapped in the towel. They walked without talking.

When they reached the boardwalk, Shauna

said, "Could I get another lesson tomorrow morning?"

"I can't," Kai said.

"Oh." Shauna gazed down with disappointment at the gray weather-beaten slats of wood that ran the length of the boardwalk. Kai felt bad for her. He knew what it was like to be stoked and unable to do anything about it.

"But another morning, okay?" he said.

She raised her head. "Sure. Thanks."

They went down the sidewalk to the corner where Kai would take a left back to the shop and Shauna would continue straight. They stopped.

"There's one other thing," Kai said. "You know that big old board in your basement? You think I could have it?"

"I'll ask my dad but I don't see why not," Shauna said.

"Think I could come by early tomorrow morning and take it?"

"I guess, but why? I thought you said it was no good."

"It isn't," Kai said. "But it could be."

Twenty-four

Kai opened his eyes. The curtain in Jade's bedroom was drawn, but around the edges he could see the dull gray light of the predawn. He turned his head. Jade was asleep beside him on the futon, her short black hair pointing in every direction. Kai drew in a deep slow breath and smelled the scent of her perfume. It was hard to leave, but he had things to do. He quietly slid off the futon and got dressed. The room was filled with colorful candles, no longer lit. But they had been last night.

An hour later he and Bean were carrying the tanker down the hill from Shauna's house. It had taken some work, but they'd managed to get the huge old surfboard out through a basement window.

"You want to carry this thing all the way to Teddy's house?" Bean complained. "Are you crazy? It weighs a ton." Kai had to admit that it was even heavier than he'd first imagined.

"Didn't you say you had a car?" Kai asked.

"Uh, yeah, but it's still in the shop," Bean said. "So what in the world does Teddy want with this hunk of junk anyway?"

"She doesn't," Kai said.

"Then why are we bringing it to her house?"

"I want her opinion of it," Kai said.

"Hey, I can give you that," Bean offered. "It feels like it's made out of concrete. You'd need a rudder to turn it on a wave. That is, if it floats. Whoever shaped it was a kook. It's a big piece of crapola. Seriously, dude, you got me up early just to show this thing to her?"

"You can't judge a book by its cover," Kai said.

"Right," Bean muttered. "Let me ask you something, Kai. Were you born this whacked or is this something that just happened recently?"

They got to Teddy's and went through the gate in the white picket fence.

"Okay, here," Kai said. He and Bean lowered the tanker to the grass outside the shed. "Thanks, Bean."

"You don't want me to stick around?" Bean asked.

Kai shook his head.

"When Teddy comes out and tells you to go to hell, how're you gonna get this thing out of here alone?"

"I'm not," Kai said.

"Right, because when Teddy sees this on her lawn, she's gonna get a gun and blow your head off."

"Later, Bean."

"I'd ask if I could have your long board, but mine's better," Bean said.

"See ya."

"Been nice knowing you, Kai." Bean went back out through the gate.

Kai went to the door of the shed and knocked. A few moments later Teddy opened the door, covered, as usual, with a fine layer of white foam dust. "What are you doing here? You know I don't have any work for you today."

"I want to ask your opinion on something," Kai said, and pointed back at the tanker lying on the grass.

"What about it?" Teddy asked.

"What do you see?" Kai asked.

"I see a very large relic squashing down part of my freshly mowed lawn, and I don't like it."

"I see a fish," Kai said.

Teddy wrinkled her nose as if something smelled bad. Kai realized he was holding his breath. If Teddy told him to go to hell, he wasn't just out of luck, he was completely screwed. She sighed, then stepped through the doorway and took a closer look at the tanker. She squatted down and lifted the tail.

"Christ, there must be twenty pounds of fiberglass on this thing," she grumbled.

"That's what I'm hoping," Kai said.

Teddy sighted down the stringer. "Okay, there's probably enough tail rocker and someone who knew what he was doing might be able to get a sufficient kicker out of it. Of course there's no way in hell to know what the condition of the foam is inside something this old." She let the tanker drop down to the grass. "Look, I don't care what you do with this thing as long as you get it off my lawn."

"Including letting me delaminate and reshape it?" Kai asked.

Teddy gave him a withering look that would have frozen the sun. "You want to use *my* shaping room?"

"You said you were gonna be glassing all next week and wouldn't be doing any shaping for a while," Kai reminded her.

"You have nerve, mister. The only person who's ever shaped a board in my shaping room is me," Teddy said. "And that's the way it's going to stay. Now get this dinosaur off my lawn before I hack it to pieces with an ax."

Teddy started back toward the shed.

"It's for a good cause," Kai said as she passed him.

She stopped. "What are you talking about?"

"I'm talking about going up against the same kind of stupid, narrow-minded thinking that stopped you from competing thirty years ago," Kai said.

Teddy stared at him the way she might have stared at a guy who'd just told her there was good surfing on the moon. "I don't know where you've been, grommet, but they now hold professional women's surfing events all over the world."

"I'm not talking about the event, I'm talking about the attitude," Kai said. "Maybe women have made progress, but the world is still filled with jerks who think women's professional surfing is a joke. And those are the same guys who think they own breaks like Screamers. I bet thirty years ago, when they didn't let you compete in the men's events, they didn't let you surf Screamers either."

Teddy's eyebrows rose. "Who have you been talking to?"

"No one," Kai answered. "It was just a guess." But from her reaction he knew he was right.

"I heard they challenged you to a heat and you backed down," she said.

"I didn't back down," Kai said. "I said I'd think about it. I figure it might help if I shape a new board while I'm thinking."

Teddy crossed her arms and looked up at the sky. A large brown-and-white hawklike bird flew overhead carrying a fish in its talons. "Osprey."

"Wasn't it once endangered but people started building roosts and now the population's back up?" Kai asked.

"I believe that's true," Teddy said.

"So people can make things change," Kai said.

Teddy looked at the tanker, then at Kai. "You better work fast because I'll be back in the shaping room a week from Monday morning, and then you're out. Any messes you make, I expect you to clean up. Any materials you use, I'm deducting from your pay. And don't even think about using any of my fin boxes or fins."

Kai smiled. "Thanks, Teddy."

Twenty-five

"**W**here were you last night?" Pat asked when Kai got to the shop.

"I stayed at a friend's house," Kai said.

"Well, well, well, look who's the big man around town," his father quipped.

"If I stay at a friend's house does that make me the big man around town?" Sean asked.

"You don't have any friends, dimwit," the Alien Frog Beast sneered.

"How do you know?" Sean asked.

"Where do you spend every day?" Pat asked him.

"Here."

"And every night?"

"Here."

"So where are all your friends?"

"I meant, *if* I had any friends," Sean said.

Pat let out an exasperated sigh. "I want you two to get up early tomorrow morning and take the truck to the city. I'll give you the address. Guy's got a load of shirts and heat transfers he wants to get rid of cheap."

"No," Kai said. He planned to start grinding down the tanker into a fish the next morning. He only had a week.

Big Chief Alien Frog Hockaloogie stared at him through the thick square glasses. "What'd you say?"

"I said I'm not going to the city tomorrow morning," Kai said.

"You're going," Pat growled. "You give me any trouble and I'll take that surfboard of yours and break it in two."

"There's no reason why we can't go in the afternoon," Kai said.

"I need you here in the store," Pat said.

"The afternoons have been dead," Kai said. "As long as it's hot and sunny everyone goes to the beach."

"Listen, sonny boy," Pat snarled, "you'll do

exactly as I say. You want to know why? Because you're dead in the water without me, understand?"

Kai frowned. It was obvious Pat thought he had something on him.

"You think I don't know about your big dream to go back to Hawaii?" Pat said. "Wake up, kid. You can't even get on an airplane. You've got no driver's license, no passport, no photo ID. You can't even prove who you are. You got a birth certificate? A social security card? An address? Any proof that you're even a citizen of the United States? You don't have diddly. You're stuck, punk."

Kai said nothing. He knew if he was quiet Pat would keep talking. And the more Pat talked, the more Kai learned.

"You're fifteen years old," his father went on. "Know what happens when the authorities find you? You become a ward of the state. Go into a foster home. And I got news for you. I don't know where that foster home's gonna be, but one thing I do know, it ain't gonna be in some nice seaside town with good surfing. Now tomorrow morning you get in that damn truck and do what I say or you'll never see Hawaii for as long as you live."

Kai stared back at his father, weighing his words. Pat could be the biggest liar in the world, but something about what he said today rang true. That didn't mean there was no hope. It just meant Kai had to chill until he figured out what to do next.

Twenty-six

The next morning Kai and Sean got in the truck and pulled out of the lot behind T-licious. They stopped at the diner and got coffee and egg sandwiches to go, then headed for the city.

"Would you really do that?" Sean asked as he drove and chewed on an egg sandwich.

"Do what?" Kai asked.

"Run away and go off on your own."

"Why not?" Kai asked.

"Wouldn't you be scared? Not knowing nobody. Not knowing what to do."

"For a little while, I guess," Kai said. "But you get to know people. And as far as what to do, that's pretty simple. You have to get some kind of job so you can afford a place to live and food to eat."

"Man, don't think I don't feel like you do sometimes," Sean said. "I get sick of that jerk bossing us around, and always telling us what to do. But I don't think I'd know what to do by myself. I don't got no friends or family except you and him."

Kai gazed out the truck's window at the roofs of the cars around them, the other trucks on the road, the grass and trees on the shoulders. No friends or family except him and Pat. That was pathetic. But it was something to think about too. If Pat ever got busted, Kai had little doubt his father would be getting an all-expenses-paid trip to the big house. One way or another, Kai knew, he could take care of himself. But where would that leave Sean?

The address Pat gave them was in Brooklyn. Tall brick buildings, asphalt streets, and sidewalks everywhere. Hardly any grass and just a couple of sickly-looking trees that seemed completely out of place in the asphalt jungle. They found the warehouse. Three young guys with shaved heads, dark Ray Bans, major tattoos, gold chains, and T-shirts were hanging around the loading dock. Kai immediately noticed that all three let their T-shirts hang untucked over their waists, where certain telltale bulges indicated the presence of weapons. Sean backed the truck into the bay and one of them strolled up.

"You duh guys here for duh T-shirts?" he asked.

"Yeah," said Sean.

"Come wit me," the guy said.

Kai and Sean got out. It felt twenty degrees hotter here in the city than it had in Sun Haven. They followed the guy through a dented metal door. Inside, the warehouse was filled with all sorts of merchandise stacked and piled haphazardly. Two dozen bed mattresses still wrapped in plastic. Twenty cases of Crest toothpaste. Boxes of DVDs. Cases of cigarettes. Piles of rugs. A whole wooden pallet of Valvoline motor oil. Boxes of women's wigs. Crates of bicycles. There was only one way to make sense of what it was all doing here. What was the phrase they used on TV? Oh, yeah, "it fell off the back of the truck."

The deal was done in cash. No invoices or receipts. No paperwork of any kind. The guys with the bulges under their T-shirts pulled open the big warehouse doors, but Sean and

Kai had to do the loading themselves. The boxes of T-shirts and heat transfers were still factory sealed, but all identifying markings, addresses, purchase orders had been torn off and no doubt shredded.

Half an hour later they were on the highway, heading home. Both Kai and Sean were covered with a film of sweat and grit from the work they'd just done.

"Man, do you believe the prices we just got?" Sean asked. "Three hundred shirts for five hundred bucks? How can they make any money on that?"

"Because it's all stolen property, Sean," Kai said. "That five hundred is pure profit for those guys."

Sean turned and stared at Kai with wide eyes. "You think?"

"Sean, they had guns in their waistbands," Kai said. "We're not exactly talking about the Better Business Bureau here."

Sean was still staring at him.

Kai cleared his throat. "Eyes on the road, okay?"

Sean looked back at the highway. "How would Dad know about things like that?"

Kai didn't know how to answer that

question. Instead he felt a sad ache for his half brother.

They rode for a long time without talking. Then Kai happened to glance over at the truck's gas gauge. It was on empty. "Hey, Sean, we're gonna run out of gas before we get back."

Sean checked the gas gauge. "Maybe not. We're probably only ten miles from home."

"Yeah, but if we do run out of gas, then what's gonna happen?" Kai asked.

"We'll have to go get some," Sean said.

"How?"

Sean blinked. "Yeah, I guess you're right. We better get off at the next exit, huh?"

The sign for the next exit said FAIRPORT. As they entered the town Kai could see that it was less of a resort area than Sun Haven. There were fewer motels and restaurants. It appeared to be more of a community of summer homes. Sean drove practically to the center of town to find a gas station.

Kai got out of the truck and stretched while Sean pumped the gas. The sun was bright and hot, but not as scalding as in Brooklyn, where it had felt like a heat furnace. Here, with a breeze, it felt toasty and comforting. Across the street from the gas station was Fairport Surf, a small shop with a couple of boards in the window. Beside the shop was a large green garbage bin, and sticking out of the bin was something Kai was suddenly very interested in.

"Be right back," he said to Sean, and went across the street for a closer look. Poking out of the bin was the bottom of a thruster. The board was broken in half—a total loss. But the three fins and fin boxes looked fine, and about the right size for his fish. This was exactly what he needed.

Kai went into the shop. The familiar scents of neoprene, resin, and surf wax were in the air. There were racks of bathing suits and trunks and rash guards. Boards, bodyboards, skim boards. Board bags and socks. Wet suits and gloves and booties and hoods. A surf movie played on a TV monitor that was bolted to the ceiling. The movie was accompanied by the familiar sounds of a guitar on overdrive.

A well-tanned girl wearing green shorts and a pink bikini top looked up from a copy of *Vogue* magazine and studied him for a moment. She had long, light brown, sun-streaked hair, green eyes, and a diamond stud in her right nostril.

"Uh, I noticed a broken board in the bin next to the shop," Kai said.

"Yeah?" said the girl.

"Any chance I could have it?"

The girl frowned. "What for?"

"The fins. I'm building a board."

"Sure." The girl shrugged, then looked back down at the magazine. Now that he was in the shop, Kai made his way to the back, where the rentals and used boards were usually kept. Perhaps, if he was amazingly lucky, he'd find a good, used, incredibly cheap short board for sale. It would save him a lot of time and work on the tanker.

Of course it was just wishful thinking. There were lots of short boards, but none that Kai could afford. He was just about to leave when he saw something out of the corner of his eye. Sitting in the rack of used long boards was a banana yellow Rennie Yater.

Kai took a closer look. He couldn't be sure, but it appeared to be just like one he had seen in Curtis's shed before all of Curtis's best boards were stolen. He ran his fingers down the rail. Most people probably wouldn't even realize what they were looking at, but this board was a piece of surfing history, and Kai wasn't surprised that the price tag said nine hundred dollars. This wasn't just a used board; it was a collectible.

Kai went back to the girl at the counter. She was probably eighteen or nineteen. "Uh, excuse me."

She looked up from the magazine. "Yes?"

"I'm curious about one of the used boards," Kai said. "That Rennie Yater?"

She scowled.

"It's in the back," Kai said.

The girl got up and came around the counter. She was tall and had a great figure. They walked to the back and Kai pointed out the board. The girl leaned it out of the rack and gave it a look.

"Wow, I didn't even know we had this," she said.

"It's a beauty, huh?" Kai said.

"It must have just come in because I'm pretty sure it wasn't here last week."

"Where do these boards come from?"

"Different places," said the girl. "Sometimes people bring them in and ask us to sell them. Sometimes Rick gets a bunch of boards, but I don't know from where."

"Rick's the owner?" Kai asked.

"Yeah."

"He around?"

"No, he works a day job and usually doesn't get here until after work."

"Okay, thanks."

"You mean, you're not going to buy it?" the girl asked with a teasing wink as she slid the Yater back into the rack. As if everyone walked around with an extra nine hundred dollars.

Kai patted his pockets. "Gee, left all my cash at home." Together, they walked toward the front of the store. Kai was aware that the girl was now checking him out.

"You from around here?" she asked.

"Sun Haven," Kai said.

"Oh, that's not so far. Where do you surf?"

"Up and down the beach."

"Screamers?"

"Once in a while."

"Sometimes my girlfriends and I go over there. Just for a change of pace, you know? Where do you hang out?"

"I work in a T-shirt shop in town," Kai said. "Usually just surf in the mornings."

"Next time we go over there, maybe we'll stop by," the girl said. Although it was more of a question than a statement.

"Sure," Kai said.

The girl smiled. "Great. See you around."

"Yeah, and thanks for the broken board," Kai said.

"Anytime."

Kai left the shop and stepped into the sunlight. He walked around to the side of the store and got the broken tail out of the bin, then headed across the street to the gas station. Sean was just coming out of the office.

"What're you gonna do with that?" Sean asked when he saw Kai with the broken thruster.

"Take off the fins," Kai said.

Without another word they got into the truck and started toward Sun Haven. Kai couldn't stop thinking about that yellow Rennie Yater. He really wanted to know where it came from. And if it was one of Curtis's, what was it doing in the Fairport Surf Shop?

Twenty-seven

The surf started to pick up again. Kai was dying to get back into the water, but he had to spend his mornings at Teddy's, stripping fiberglass and planing the tanker down to a fish. When he was nearly finished mowing foam, Teddy came into the shaping room and studied the result.

"Guess you haven't shaped many boards, huh?" she said after looking it over.

"Actually, this is the first one I've ever tried," Kai said, pulling off the ventilation mask and wiping some damp white foam dust off his forehead.

"Really? It's not bad for the first time," Teddy said. "You may actually have some talent."

"Thanks," Kai said.

"Don't thank me," Teddy replied, bending down and giving the board a closer look. "I said you *may* have some talent. But believe me, this won't be remembered as your finest work. For one thing, your rails are a little thin. In fact, the whole thing looks a little thin to me."

"I want to go as light as I can," Kai explained.

Teddy dragged a finger across the deck. "That you did, only this isn't a fish anymore, it's a potato chip made out of thirty-year-old foam."

"Shouldn't matter," Kai said.

Teddy arched an eyebrow, clearly saying he didn't know what he was talking about.

"I'll tell you what'll matter," she said. "Your edge is too soft. And I don't see enough nose rocker here for dropping in late on anything more than a waist-high wave. You really want to ride this in a heat?"

"I don't have a choice," Kai said.

"I heard that you don't even need to do this to get a spot in the Screamers lineup," Teddy said as she continued to study the board from different angles. "They'd probably let you in just because you've made it clear that you're not going to go away no matter who runs you down. You know, 'If you can't beat 'em, you might as well let 'em join you.'"

Now it was Kai's turn to trace the board's rail with his fingertips. Was there enough foam left to harden the edge?

"So seriously, why are you doing this?" Teddy asked. Something about her tone was different. The tough-lady sarcasm wasn't there. "Why put yourself through all this work and trouble when all you have to do is paddle out?"

"I think that anyone should be able to surf Screamers," Kai said.

"You'd have mayhem out there," Teddy said.

Kai looked up from the board. "I'm surprised to hear you say that. I mean, you of all people."

"It was different thirty years ago," Teddy said. "The reason they wouldn't let me into the lineup had nothing to do with it being too crowded. They were just a bunch of macho chauvinist pigs and I was a girl who could rip. Just between you and me, I think some of them were scared that I'd look better out there than they did. Now it's different.

They may still be chauvinist pigs, but it's not girls they're scared of. It's the traffic jam."

"Maybe traffic jams are the cost of freedom," Kai said. "I don't know. I just don't think it's right for anyone to say this break or that break is theirs and no one else can surf it. You really think the ancient Hawaiians ran guys down?"

"No, I don't think there were that many of them, and they had plenty of waves and plenty of room to surf," Teddy said. "I mean, in a sense they were all locals back then. It's not like today when every grem with a few bucks can buy a board and paddle out. I admire your beliefs, Kai; I just don't happen to think they're very realistic."

"Just because a grem can paddle doesn't mean he's gonna paddle out to Screamers," Kai said. "First of all, the better surfers are gonna get the waves earlier and any grem who drops in on them gets read the riot act. So now what's he gonna do? Just float out there all day long watching other guys catch waves? No, he's gonna move over to Sewers or find another spot where there's room to learn."

Teddy picked up a rasp and carefully worked it along the board's rail. "So you're determined to ride this thing in a heat against Sam?"

"I'm sure thinking about it," Kai said.

"What about fins?"

By now Kai had cut the fin boxes out of the broken thruster he'd found outside Fairport Surf. Teddy looked at them, then back at the fish. "Close enough," she said.

"That's what I thought," said Kai.

"One last thing," Teddy said. "You even know anything about competing?"

"Enough," Kai said.

Twenty-eight

The first ninety-degree days of June arrived. On TV they were calling it an early-summer heat wave. By noon the sidewalks were scalding, and you could smell the scent of tar melting in the street. The T-shirt shop got quiet. All the shoppers had fled to pools and the beach. Pat went out and left Sean and Kai to mind the store. Not that there was much to mind. Sean sat in the back office watching TV and playing video games on the computer. Kai stayed in the front, sketching out possible air brush designs for the fish. He'd pretty much finished shaping it, and now it was a question of whether he wanted to paint it before glassing it.

The front door opened and Pat came in

sipping Mountain Dew through a straw from a huge thirty-two-ounce plastic cup. His forehead gleamed and there were dark sweat stains around his collar and arm pits.

"Hotter than a witch's tit out there," he grumbled. Kai didn't bother to point out that as far as he knew, the saying was "colder than a witch's tit."

"Only places doing any business are the ice-cream shop, the convenience store, and that surf store," Pat said. "What're all those kids doing in that place on a day like this? How come they're not out surfing?"

"The surf's probably been blown out by the onshore thermals," Kai said. He didn't bother to add that it didn't hurt Buzzy Frank's business to have a babe like Jade behind the counter for all the grems and groms to sneak looks at.

"So if they can't surf, those kids hang out in that store lookin' at surfboards and crap," Pat said. "And maybe they see a T-shirt they like and they buy it. Tell you what. Go through the books and see what they got about surfing. I'm thinking maybe we'll do a little display in the window."

Kai pulled out one of the catalogs and

started to thumb through it. He was kind of curious to see what they had in the way of heat transfers for surfing. If he found any, he would choose the ugliest and most unappealing transfers possible. Pat would never know the difference. Meanwhile, hyped on countless cups of coffee chased with Mountain Dew, Pat slithered around the store like a caged cobra.

Kai found the section on surf heat transfers and was trying to decide between the pig on the surfboard or the duck on a surfboard when Pat announced he was going back out again.

"I'll be back after dinner," he said.

Take as much time as you like, thought Kai.

Around five thirty Shauna, Bean, and Booger came in together.

"Where've you been, dude?" Bean asked.

"I've had stuff to do," Kai said. "What's going on?"

"You know the surf's been slowly building the last few days?" Bean said. "With this heat wave it's blown out by ten every morning. But early this morning it was waist high. Everybody thought you'd be out there."

"Who's everybody?" Kai asked, puzzled.

"You know. Boogs and me. Sam even paddled over to Sewers and said something."

"Let me guess," Kai said. "He misses my companionship."

"They all say you chickened out," Booger said.

Kai shrugged. "Let 'em think that if they like."

"You're not really gonna chicken out, are you?" Booger asked. "I mean, you gotta surf against him or everyone's gonna think you're a wuss."

Kai had to smile. "Know what I like about you, Booger? You always tell it like it is. So let me ask you something. Did you ever wonder how we got to the point where people surf *against* each other? I mean, what happened to surfing *with* each other? You know, going out there and sitting together waiting for the waves. A set comes in and one of you takes one. Then the other guy goes. Maybe you even wind up paddling back out together. No one's trying to beat anybody. No one's trying to beat anyone up. It's just this nice, peaceful, enjoyable experience."

"In your dreams," Bean said.

Kai looked at Shauna, who raised and lowered her shoulders as if she didn't know who was right.

"You guys hear what happened to Curtis?" Kai asked. "Someone broke into his shed and stole all his best boards."

"Bummer," said Booger.

Kai leaned over the counter and spoke in a lower voice. "Here's what's really strange. I was coming back from the city in the truck the other day and we had to stop in Fairport for gas. So there's a small surf shop in town—"

"Fairport Surf," Bean said.

"You know it?" Kai asked.

"It's where I got my first board. It's not easy to find a decent used long board around here," Bean said. "I used to go up and down the coast once a week stopping in all the shops to see if anything good had come in."

Kai continued with his story: "I went into Fairport Surf to check the place out and there was this beautiful used Rennie Yater in there that looked just like one I saw in Curtis's shed a few weeks ago."

"Did you ask the owner where he got it?" Shauna asked.

"He wasn't there," Kai said. "But the girl at the counter said it must have come in recently because she didn't remember seeing it the week before."

"You should have copied down the serial number on the stringer," Bean said.

"Why? You think Curtis ever wrote them down?" Kai asked.

Bean rubbed the end of his long black braid between his fingers as if he was thinking. "You're right. He's not the type to do something like that. So there'd be no way to know for certain that it was his board, and not just another used Yater."

"Did you tell Curtis about it?" Shauna asked.

"No way," Kai said. "The guy's kind of unstable, you know? The first time he found me in his backyard he pulled a sawed-off shotgun on me. I can just see him going into Fairport Surf with that gun and demanding the board back. The thing is, having those boards stolen is the lowest blow ever for him. He's talking about selling the Driftwood and leaving. We gotta help the guy out."

"People in town would love to take a wrecking ball to Curtis's place," Bean said. "They've been trying to get rid of him for years."

"So, what are you gonna do about Screamers?" Booger asked, as if that was the only thing that really mattered.

"You really want me to surf against Sam, huh?" Kai asked.

"Are you kidding?" Booger said. "I am so ready to step into the greenroom. I fricken dream about it."

Bean patted Booger on the shoulder. "Simple minds beget simple desires."

Booger pulled back. "What's that mean?"

"It basically means you're right," Bean said. "We'd all love to get tubed at Screamers."

Kai still had to finish glassing the fish. But now that he was done using Teddy's shaping room, that could wait a day. He still had #43, the long board Curtis had given him, and he was pretty eager to get back into the water.

"Okay," he said. "I'll see you guys in the morning."

"You're going to do it?" Shauna asked. "You're going to surf against Sam?"

"I don't know," Kai said. "I couldn't tomorrow morning even if I wanted to, because my new board's not ready. But I'll bring down my long board just to see what's going on."

Twenty-nine

The surf was knee to waist high the next morning and an early easterly breeze made it bumpy and irregular. Kai almost regretted spending the past few mornings in Teddy's shaping room when he could have been surfing in better conditions. It was the classic surfing story—"Ya should have been here yesterday."

Just as he had the week before, he spent the first half hour of the dawn sharing Screamers with Buzzy and Lucas Frank. Once again Buzzy was pushing his son hard to make the best of the sloppy conditions. Kai was glad to be on #43, but at the same time, he kept wondering what it would be like to ride the fish once it was glassed and ready.

Sam and Everett were the next surfers to arrive. Both paddled out to Screamers. This was the first time Kai and Sam had been in the water together since Sam ran Kai down and put that gash in #43. Sitting on the long board farther outside than the others, Kai wondered if Sam would try anything today. He was surprised when Sam and Everett paddled out to him. Clearly this was a "social" visit. There was no way those guys were going to catch waves on their short boards from that far out.

"How's the chicken of the sea, tuna?" Sam asked with a nasty leer.

"You still think I'm afraid to surf against you?" Kai asked.

"Any reason for me not to think that?" Sam asked.

"Maybe because I'm on a long board and there's no way a long board can compete with a short board. That is, unless you want to hold that heat in conditions like these."

The lines in Sam's forehead bunched up. Today's conditions were barely surfable on a short board. "No way."

"Now who's chicken?" Kai asked.

Everett smirked. Sam's face colored and his

eyes became slits of anger. "I wouldn't surf here today if I were you."

"Or what?" Kai asked.

"You'll see."

Kai turned to Everett. "Think you could leave us alone for a second?"

Everett paddled away and Kai got on his knees and paddled closer to Sam. When he got really close, he spoke in a low voice: "You try to run me down today and I'll take that leash and wrap it around your neck so tight your eyes'll pop right out of your skull. And I'll do it *before* one of your friends grabs me from behind and stops me."

Sam gritted his teeth, but said nothing. One of the larger sets of the morning was coming in and Kai turned his board around and started to paddle. He gave Sam a look, more or less letting him know that this was a perfect time to make a move if he was stupid enough to try. Sam didn't budge. Kai caught the wave. Ahead of him, Lucas was paddling his short board into the same wave, but Kai didn't think it was an intentional drop in. Lucas might not have seen him.

"Comin' down," Kai said, just loud enough to be heard.

Lucas jerked his head around in surprise and instantly sat back on his board, pulling out of the wave. Just as Kai had suspected, he didn't realize someone else was already on it.

At the same time, Buzzy gave him a seriously bad-ass vibe as Kai cruised past switchfoot so that they'd be face-to-face. Looked like the local attitude had definitely been passed down along family lines.

Kai kicked out of the wave and started to paddle back. Out of the corner of his eye he watched Sam catch a wave and start to gash and thrash. The guy's sole intention appeared to be hitting the lip as hard as he could and sending spray as high as possible. He was like a baseball player swinging for home runs on every pitch.

Moments later Lucas caught a wave in that set, so when Kai got back outside, the only one there was Everett. They nodded at each other as they watched for the next set.

"I hear it was pretty nice yesterday," Kai said.

The lines between Everett's eyebrows bunched briefly, as if he wasn't sure how to deal with this. "They were okay," he answered. "I was kind of hoping they'd keep building overnight, but it didn't happen."

"What do you hear about the next few days?" Kai asked.

"Supposed to get better. Maybe head high or bigger by the end of the week." For a moment it seemed as if Everett would say more, but then he looked past Kai and grew quiet. Kai didn't have to look around to know that Sam had paddled back out.

When Kai did look, he found Runt, not Sam, sitting on his board about ten feet away. The red-haired kid gave Kai his toughest bad-ass look. "So big talker, you just gonna talk forever, or you finally gonna walk the walk and show us what you got? 'Cause I think it's all a lot of hot air."

It was becoming painfully obvious to Kai that he had no choice. Either he'd have to compete or spend the rest of his stay in Sun Haven listening to this garbage. "I hear it might get to head high by the end of the week," he said. "If that happens, the heat's on."

Runt turned to the others. Sam was paddling out and Lucas was sitting in the waves with his father about fifteen yards away. "Hey, guys, guess what?" he called. "Next head-high day, it's a go."

Lucas glanced at Kai, then nodded. Kai

suddenly realized that if he wanted to have the fish ready to surf by the end of the week, he had better do some glassing today. About two hundred yards down the beach, he saw Bean and Shauna crossing the boardwalk and hitting the sand. He caught the next decent wave in.

"Sam try to run you down today?" Bean asked when he saw Kai carrying his board up the beach.

"Naw, he behaved himself," Kai said. He looked at Shauna, dressed in that big old wet suit and carrying a bodyboard and fins. "This would be a good day to practice on a board."

Shauna made a face. "If only I had one."

"Want to use mine?"

"Could I?"

"Sure, just leave it by the door at the back of the shop when you're finished."

"You're not gonna surf anymore today?" Bean asked.

"I have to go take care of something," Kai said.

"You couldn't have gotten much surf time in this morning," Bean said. "It was still dark an hour ago."

"I have to keep glassing my new board if

I'm gonna be ready to surf against Sam by the end of the week."

Bean's mouth fell open with surprise. "You—you're gonna—you decided to do it?"

"I don't want to, but I don't see that I have a choice," Kai said.

Thirty

Kai jogged up the beach and across the boardwalk. He figured that if he hurried he'd have time to go back to the shop, change out of the wet suit, go over to Teddy's and work on the fish for a few hours, then get back to the shop in time for it to open. Ahead of him, Jade was coming down the sidewalk in a T-shirt and shorts. They both stopped.

"Hi, stranger," she said. "Where's your board?"

"Lent it to a friend. Where's yours?"

"I didn't come down here to surf," Jade said. "I was looking for this nice younger guy I recently spent some time with."

"Anyone I know?" Kai asked.

Jade smiled. "So, haven't seen you around much."

"Sorry, I've been really busy," Kai said.

She rolled her eyes. "Come on, Kai, at least give me a line I haven't heard before."

"It's true."

"You don't strike me as the type who loves 'em and leaves 'em," she said.

"Nope. Just loves 'em," Kai said.

Jade reached up and pulled a strand of seaweed out of his hair. "Then maybe I'll be seeing you again, huh?"

"Sounds good. But seriously, Jade, I've got to book."

Jade pulled him close and kissed him hard on the lips, then pushed him away. "No problem. I love a good book."

Kai spent the rest of that morning, and the next few mornings after that, working on the new board. Just as Everett had predicted, the surf steadily increased in size. As it did, the parking lot at the Driftwood Motel began to fill with a motley collection of surfboard-transporting vehicles. Kai noticed more young men—and some young women—around town. Sometimes, early in the morning on the way to Teddy's, he'd pass some guys sleeping in a car with out-of-state plates and boards on top, and he'd know they'd driven all night just to be able to surf on their day off. Once or twice he came across an empty six-pack and some empty bottles and cans left on the sidewalk—something Buzzy Frank and the city fathers wouldn't exactly be thrilled with.

Finally one morning Kai put the gloss coat on. It was getting late and the resin needed time to cure. Kai would have to wait until the next day to do the final sanding, buffing, and polishing. With less than an hour until he had to be at the store, he decided to walk down to the beach to check out the surf.

He heard it before he saw it: The louder-than-normal crashing, sounding like distant thunder. A block from the beach he saw wisps of white spray shooting high into the air beyond the dunes and shrubs. Without a doubt this was the biggest surf Sun Haven had seen since he'd arrived.

The parking lot next to the boardwalk was filled with vans, pickups, and sedans with empty surf racks. Some of the license plates were from beyond neighboring states, a sign that surfers had come from far and wide to get on the waves. When he reached the boardwalk,

Kai got his first real look. The waves were easily shoulder high, maybe higher, peeling nicely right to left with only occasional sectioning. The kind of day that made Kai ache to be out there.

From the boardwalk Kai counted more surfers in the water than he'd seen in all the previous weeks combined. Even Screamers was more crowded than usual. In addition to Lucas's regular crew, Buzzy Frank was actively surfing, along with Dave McAllister, Jade, and a few others Kai recognized from Sun Haven Surf. Several more were probably older, "honorary past members" of the local crew, who now only surfed when the conditions were better than average.

A hundred yards to the right, another bunch of surfers sat outside Sewers. Kai spotted Bean and Booger among them. A medium-size set came in and an older guy positioned his long board perfectly and took off with one effortless stroke of his arms. He was the only one out there not wearing a wet suit and Kai quickly saw why. The older guy popped up gracefully, turned the board into the curl, walked to the nose and stood with his hands loosely clasped behind him, looking ahead like the captain of a ship standing in the bow. It was as remarkable a show of grace and experience as Kai had seen since Hawaii, and he had to laugh at himself for not realizing sooner who it had to be. It was Curtis, showing everyone how it was done.

Kai walked down the beach. Shauna was sitting on the sand, wearing shorts and a T-shirt, her knees pulled up under her chin.

"How come you're not out there?" Kai asked, sitting down next to her.

"Oh, hi!" Shauna flashed him a surprised grin. "Are you serious? It's way too big for me. How come *you're* not out there?"

"I had to get some work done this morning," Kai said. "And now I don't have time before I go to the shop."

"Bet you wish you were surfing," she said.

"Oh, yeah." Kai's eyes were on the guys at Screamers. Some of them were actually getting tubed for short distances. Jade got one that Kai was sure was going to close down on her, and he was both surprised and delighted when she suddenly popped out, both arms raised in triumph. Very little could make Kai feel envious, but coming out of a barrel like that was definitely up there.

"How can that old guy surf without a wet suit?" Shauna brought Kai's attention back to the scene in front of them. Curtis was on his knees paddling back out. Despite the size of the surf, he nimbly picked his way through it without needing to turn turtle or even punch through very hard.

"That's Curtis," Kai said. "Owns the Driftwood Motel."

"The one they stole the boards from?"

"Right."

"Is he paddling on his knees to keep from getting wet?"

"That's the way they used to do it back in the days before they had wet suits. Guys like him could stay out there all day and hardly get a drop on them."

"Amazing."

"Oh, yeah. Those guys were tremendous surfers. All-around watermen."

They watched the others catch waves. Here and there someone got some air or produced a really stylish snap or cutback. A couple of long boarders got five on the nose. There were plenty of good surfers out there, but even in that crowd, Curtis stood out, catching more waves than anyone else and riding them with the natural grace that came only with so many years and so many waves.

Finally the older man rode in. Even on a relatively "big" day for Sun Haven, it probably never occurred to him to use a leash. In the shallows he tucked the board under his bare arm and walked up the beach, limping slightly and changing directions when he noticed Kai waving at him.

"Gee, old man, I didn't know you still surfed," Kai joked.

"Once in a while." Curtis smiled as he stood his board up in the sand.

"You looked good out there. How come you came in?"

"Water's a little bit chillier than I thought," Curtis said. "Either that or I'm just gettin' wimpy in my old age."

"But you hardly got wet," Shauna said.

"The legs feel it, and the body gets the spray," Curtis said. "Like a cold shower out there today. My guess is the Gulf Stream must be a little farther offshore than usual because that water's suddenly gotten nippy."

"Where'd you get the board?" Kai asked.

"This?" Curtis shrugged. "A marginal old stick from the backyard collection. I'd still like to know who took my good boards. I ever find that son of a bitch, I'll make sure the SOB spends the rest of his life dead."

Kai felt himself grin. It was good to see Curtis being feisty again.

"So, grommet, I hear you're gonna give up your principles and compete," Curtis said.

"No choice, old man," Kai said.

"There's always a choice," Curtis said.

Kai jerked his head toward the bunch at Screamers. "Yeah, the choice is to let those guys go on owning that break forever."

"A couple of days ago they were gonna let you in," Curtis said.

"What about Bean and Booger and the others?" Kai asked.

"Maybe they have to do what you did," Curtis said. "Go over there and show that they're not gonna back down no matter what the dickheads try."

"It's not right," Kai said.

"Listen, grom, take some advice from an old fart who's surfed more breaks than that whole crew combined. There are some things in life you can't change. Maybe you can change who's in the lineup, but you'll never change the way those guys think. What the hell are you gonna ride against Sam anyway?"

"I got a fish," Kai said.

"From where?"

"Made it myself."

Curtis's bushy eyebrows rose. "My, you are one resourceful young grommet. You're tellin' me Teddy actually let you use her shaping room?"

Kai nodded.

"May wonders never cease," Curtis said. "So when's this great big heat going to take place?"

"Soon as the swell gets to head high or better."

Curtis turned and gazed out at the horizon. It almost seemed to Kai like he was sniffing the air. "I expect that will be tomorrow morning, grom."

"Then that's when it'll be."

"And where is this wonderful homemade board of yours?" Curtis asked.

"Still curing at Teddy's."

Curtis cocked his head and looked at Kai like he was crazy. "You're gonna go up against Sam on a homemade board you've never ridden before? Boy, maybe I should have shot you the day I found you in my yard. Put you out of your misery."

"Think you might come down tomorrow morning?" Kai asked. "I'd really appreciate it if you were there."

"Hell, yes," Curtis said. "They ain't fed slaves to the lions since the Roman Empire. I wouldn't miss this for the world." He picked up his board and limped off down the beach toward the Driftwood.

Thirty-one

It might have been Kai's imagination, but it seemed like an unusual number of kids came into T-licious that day. More than once he caught some gremmie staring at him. At first Pat seemed pleased by all the extra traffic, which he assumed was because of the new surfing-duck-and-pig T-shirt display in the window. But he grew increasingly annoyed as he realized that no one was buying T-shirts. In fact, most of the kids didn't even look at what was hanging on the racks and draped on the walls.

"What's wrong with these kids?" he complained after a group of girls came in, stared at Kai, whispered among themselves, then left without so much as looking at a shirt.

"They're coming to see Kai, not the shirts," Sean said.

Pat pursed his lips. "Maybe we ought to sell you," he said to Kai. "We could rent you out for an hour at a time."

"What about me?" Sean asked.

Pat groaned. "We'd have to pay people to take you."

Around lunchtime Bean and Booger came in.

"How was it out there today?" Kai asked.

"Fun, but a little scary," Bean said. "When it gets big like this we get some serious rip currents. I heard the lifeguards have been saving people all day long."

"And it's cold," Booger added. "Felt like the water temp must've dropped five degrees last night."

"Curtis said something about the Gulf Stream moving offshore," Kai said.

"Also, you get this steady offshore breeze for a couple of days and it blows away the surface water," Bean said.

"So the heat's really tomorrow?" Booger asked.

"Looks like it," Kai said.

"Who're you gonna use for judges?" Booger asked.

"I was thinking of you two," Kai said.

Booger looked shocked. "But I don't know nothing about judging a surf contest."

"It won't matter," Kai said.

"Huh? Why not?"

"Just be there, okay?"

"Okay."

Kai pointed at the new display in the front window. "So what do you think of our new surfing display?"

Bean leaned close, bridging the counter. "Frankly, I'm not sure I've ever seen two uglier T-shirts."

That brought a smile to Kai's lips. "Thank you, Bean."

"Hey!" Pat came over and interrupted them. "You two got business here?"

Bean and Booger backed away from the counter.

"We were just talking to Kai," Booger said.

"Well, Kai's busy," Pat said. "So unless you wanna buy something, I suggest you take your business elsewhere."

Kai was tempted to tell Pat to shove off, but he knew that would cause trouble, and he already had plans for that evening that were going to get him into enough trouble. So instead he gave his friends a nod. "Catch you later, dudes."

Bean and Booger left. Kai spent the rest of the afternoon in the shop. Just before dinnertime the door opened, and Lucas and Sam strolled in.

"Classy joint," Lucas said, glancing around.

"Can I help you?" Kai asked.

"Looks like we're on for tomorrow morning, huh?" Sam said.

"Fine with me," said Kai.

"Six thirty?"

Kai nodded.

"You have your two judges?" Lucas asked.

"Uh-huh."

"How about a board?" Sam asked.

"That's not your problem," Kai said. "I said I'd be there."

Sam glowered at Kai. This close, Kai could see the big guy's pulse throbbing under the black barbwire tattoo around his neck.

"Come on, let's go." Lucas clapped his hand on Sam's shoulder, but Sam shrugged it off and glared at Kai. "You're going down, punk."

Kai waved. "Tomorrow morning."

Thirty-two

Each night around dinnertime Pat gave Kai five bucks and fifteen minutes to get something to eat. That night Kai ate and then headed for Teddy's house. There was no point in telling the Alien Frog Beast ahead of time that he wouldn't be coming back to work that evening because his father would never have agreed.

At Teddy's, Kai picked up the fish and changed into his wet suit, which he'd stashed there the day before. Then he headed for the beach.

By normal standards, the fish wasn't ready to be surfed yet. It had not been finely sanded, buffed, or polished. But given the choice between getting used to an unfinished board tonight or riding a finished board for the first time in the heat tomorrow, Kai preferred the former.

It was a half hour before sunset and only a few surfers were out. The waves were chest high or better, crashing like artillery rounds. Now that the sun's rays were weakening, a sea mist from the exploding foam hung in the air. While the onshore thermals blew out the surf most mornings by eleven, and by midafternoon the surf was a disorganized mishmash, usually in the late evening the winds calmed down briefly. And even though it was rarely as smooth and clean as it was in the morning, it was often rideable.

Kai put the board down and yanked on his wet suit, then kneeled in the sand and pulled out two bars of wax, one hard and the other soft. He rubbed the hard wax on the deck first, to act as a base coat, then rubbed the soft wax over it for the traction he'd need in the cold water. Then he picked up the board and headed in.

The chill of the water caught Kai by surprise. Booger was right. It had to be at least five degrees colder than just a few days before.

Still used to the buoyancy of #43, it took Kai a moment to adjust to the smaller board. Paddling out was a lot more like swimming with a kickboard under his chest, but the good news was that it was a lot easier to duck dive under the breaking waves. And when the waves were this big, that was a real advantage. It wasn't long before he was outside, straddling the board with only its pointed nose visible above the surface.

The sun was low in the sky. Sitting on the board just outside the break, Kai rose and fell with each passing swell. The waves rolling past were the biggest Kai had seen yet. Even bigger than that morning. As they passed they reminded Kai of moving blue-green mountains. It took power to move waves like that. The kind of power that could really hammer a surfer if he found himself in the impact zone.

Kai felt a shiver. Being on the fish, he sat deeper in the chilly water. It was time to stop admiring nature and see what this new stick could do.

The broad open lines of a new set were approaching, and Kai paddled over to it. The first two waves rumbled past like trains. Kai paddled into the third, only to see it roll past beneath him. He looked over his shoulder for the next wave in the set and found it looming over him like a dark blue cliff, the lip already beginning to feather and crackle.

Aw, crap . . .

The wave thundered down. Thankfully it wasn't quite pitched enough to throw him over the falls, but it was more than willing to dump several thousand pounds of water on him and send him flailing beneath the roiling surface like a doll in a washing machine. Kai didn't bother to struggle. He'd been in enough hold downs to know better. Instead he just kept his arms over his head, in case he banged into the board, and let the water pummel him. Then, when he felt the energy of the wave dissipate, he popped up to the surface and caught a breath just before the fifth wave in the set crashed down and he was once again thrashed.

The next time Kai came up for air, he was in a vast pool of swirling white soup. He quickly looked toward the horizon. Luckily there were no more big waves in the set to maul him. Next he turned toward shore to look for his board and saw it floating on the surface about halfway in. Muttering angrily to himself, he started to swim toward it. There wasn't much light left, and he still hadn't caught a wave.

Kai grabbed the fish, turned, and paddled out again. To the west, the setting orange sun was only a semicircle over the distant beach houses. The clouds in the sky were turning pink and purple, and the mist had become a drifting pink-orange haze. Kai knew he would be lucky to find time for two more rides before the light was gone entirely.

Fortune was with him. No sooner had he gotten out than a new set came in. Kai jumped on the first good wave, hit the bottom, dug his toeside rail in, and turned hard up the face. For an instant the board was vertical, the pleasure of weightlessness catching him by surprise. *Man, how long has it been?* With the lip looming above, half a dozen possibilities fired through his mind. *Easy does it,* he decided, coming up into a floater. *One step at a time.* The wave closed out in front of him and Kai dropped down into the foam. He quickly turned the board around and headed back out to catch another one.

The sun was below the horizon now and the pink and purple clouds overhead were darkening quickly. Kai paddled into a wave. This time going backside, then switchfoot, trying for a roundhouse he already knew he wouldn't be able to make. *It's okay,* he thought as the attempt stalled and left him, for a split second, sliding backward down the face of the wave before it folded over him. He had to make mistakes if he was going to figure out what he and the board were capable of. Next time he would compress more, pull his lead shoulder around with greater force, push down harder with his back foot.

The good news was he held on to his board in the suds. It was almost too dark now to judge the size and speed of the approaching waves, but a nearly three-quarter moon had begun to rise out of the southeast. Kai had been so busy keeping an eye on the sunset that he hadn't noticed it before, but now it sat just above the horizon, casting an ever widening path of white sparkles across the water toward him.

In the last embers of sunlight and the rising glimmer of moonlight, Kai paddled back out for one more wave. This time he had to wait. Only then did he realize how cold he was. In fact he'd begun shivering. Teeth chattering, he squeezed his hands into the armpits of the wet suit. Those hands were now so cold he wondered if they'd slide numbly off the board's deck when he tried to push up to his feet. But there was no question in his mind about going in yet. This last ride wouldn't be about testing either the board or himself. It was for the pure joy of riding a wave. So he stayed out there in the dark, waiting, hoping, praying for one more. Not wanting to leave just yet.

As if the ocean understood what Kai craved, it sent him a beauty. It began as a long dark line rising out of the horizon, and Kai felt a smile grow on his face in pace with the approaching monster. It was going to be the wave of the day, and he paddled into position, turned the nose of his board around, and got ready to catch it.

After what felt like the right interval, Kai looked over his shoulder, expecting to see the wave looming up over him.

But it wasn't there.

It was still thirty feet behind him.

For a second Kai didn't understand. Based on the other sets that had come through, this wave should have been there by now. But as he felt the water's surface tightening around him, he realized what had happened. He'd misjudged. In the darkness his depth perception had been fooled. The wave hadn't yet arrived because it was larger than he'd thought. Much larger. He could feel himself being drawn backward as the massive behemoth pulled thousands of gallons up its face. A dark, ominous shadow fell over him as the rising mountain of water blocked the moonlight. Kai knew instantly that there was no possible way he could get over it or punch through. He felt a jolt—the sudden energy of self-preservation—as if he'd just been given a huge injection of adrenaline, and started to kick and paddle as hard as he could.

The monster rose behind him like a black specter. In the almost pitch-black shadow, Kai dug and kicked with all his might. If he caught this thing it was going to be the ride of the summer. Possibly a standing-room tube. From behind and above him came crackling splatters of water, sounding almost like electricity. Kai kept digging. He was almost vertical now, looking down the face into the black trough below, waiting to feel gravity catch him and begin to propel him forward and downward.

The crackling splatters grew louder. Louder . . .

Kai heard a rumble . . . a roar . . .

He felt the back of the board rise.

And in that instant he knew he was toast.

Thirty-three

Only once before in his life had Kai gone over the falls. It was back in Kauai—the last time he'd surfed before being shipped to the mainland. It had been a big hairy day, even by Hanalei standards. Huge waves crashing with beach-shaking thunder. Explosions of white water and foam as high as the tops of the palms. Experienced surfers standing on the shore, shaking their heads and saying it was crazy to even try. But to Kai it had represented the chance he believed he needed to prove himself. He imagined himself in a real honest-to-God stand-up tube getting blown out the mouth with the spit like at Pipeline, arms raised in triumphant fists while the crowd on the shore cheered and hooted.

There was a lineup out at Tunnels that he wanted to get into. At the age of thirteen it had seemed like the most important thing in his life. They were mostly older guys. Bigger guys. They'd laugh when he said he wanted to surf with them. But now he imagined ripping through that huge barrel and being welcomed by each and every one.

His mom's boyfriend, Ethan, was there that day and told him not to do it, but Kai wouldn't listen. The last words he ever said to Ethan were, "You're not my father."

He paddled out in the channel, then around, behind where the enormous swells were breaking on the reef. He'd never been in waves like these before. They were the size of houses and roared past at speeds he'd never seen waves travel. They made eerie hissing sounds he'd never heard waves make before.

He was scared shitless. But he'd read all the articles in the magazines. Big wave surfers were always scared the first time. Sometimes they were still scared the hundredth time. Being scared didn't matter. Catching the wave did.

He tried and tried, but every wave simply lifted him over its head and rolled under. Soon the feeling of fright was replaced by feelings of frustration and humiliation. What did he have to do to catch one of these suckers?

The only thing he could think of was what had worked on smaller waves. Start closer to the peak. Start earlier. Paddle harder.

He went for a wave and the next thing he knew he was upside down. Defying gravity until gravity and a hundred tons of water slammed him down.

He bounced off the bottom like a human basketball being dribbled by the hand of God. Having the air knocked out of his lungs like a balloon under an elephant's foot. He recalled being pummeled by wave after wave until he didn't know which way was up. His young body flailing around like a doll in a tornado. To this day he didn't know how he managed to survive and not drown.

Later it would be reported in the papers that the beating went on for nearly two minutes until another surfer managed to grab him, holding him in one arm and his surfboard in the other and letting the waves hurl them both toward shore.

He vaguely remembered hands grasping his limp arms and yanking him out of the water. People yelling. Hands carrying him up the beach. The taste of blood in his mouth. So many sharp, searing pains that it was impossible to figure out where they were all coming from. But one in particular between his neck and shoulder. Feeling the hot sand against his back. Snippets of hurried, anxious exclamations, questions, shouts. His head feeling wetter than it should have out of the water. Soft material like from a T-shirt being pressed against his skull. Fingers prodding his arms and legs, a voice asking if this or that hurt. Then a finger touched his shoulder and the pain was so unbearable he screamed.

Hands were carrying him again. The stale dry broiling air inside a car on a hot day. A flash of Ethan's face. The ovenlike heat rising up from the backseat and through the towel they'd laid out for him. Voices telling him he'd be okay. The pressure of someone pressing that soft wet cloth against his head. The sagging beige material hanging from the ceiling of the car.

Then more hands lifting him. His back on the firm, slightly scratchy sheets of a hospital gurney. Belts around his legs and chest. Squeaky wheels. The sudden chill of air-conditioning. Fluorescent lights. The sensation of being propelled forward while lying on his back. The clinking screech of a curtain being closed. The belts undone. Hands sliding him onto another set of stiff sheets, this time a bed. By now the sources of the pain becoming more distinct. His head. His shoulder. Right leg. Knee. Ankle. A woman with dark skin and jet-black hair leaning over him, saying, "This is going to sting a little bit."

It took 163 stitches to close up his head. There was a long discussion about a skin graft to cover his entire right knee and outside of his right ankle, but the doctors decided to see whether the skin would grow back on its own. The broken collarbone would heal. The chipped tooth could be capped.

The following day came the most awful news imaginable.

And with it a wound that could never, ever heal.

Thirty-four

Now in the dark one hundred and fifty yards off Sun Haven Beach, Kai once again felt himself being hurled through turbulent water. The difference between that day in Hanalei and now was that then it had been daylight and there'd been people on the beach who saw what had happened.

Now it was dark and there was no one.

This wasn't about being thrashed, it was about being mashed.

It wasn't about having hundreds of pounds of water dumped on you either. It was about being dumped yourself, along with all that water. You weren't under the waterfall. You *were* the waterfall.

Fighting wasn't an option. The only thing to hold on to was your breath.

He hit the bottom with his shoulder, then did an elongated back flip as if someone was pulling him by the ankles around a giant tire. Then he was whipped down again like a blanket being flung out over a bed. Expecting at any instant to be smashed face first into the bottom, he felt his body come to an abrupt stop and then spin wildly, only it felt as if his legs were going in one direction and the rest of his torso in the other. More contortions followed, his body being twisted, spun, stretched, yanked, and beaten by forces far, far beyond his ability to resist. There was no point in trying to open his eyes. The water was as dark as the sky above. He was totally at the mercy of the wave.

His body felt chilled, but his lungs were burning. Being tumbled over and over in the liquid dark, it was almost impossible to figure out which way was up, but he knew he had to get there soon. When he popped to the surface, it was almost by accident. As if the ocean knew what he needed, it gave him barely enough time to grab a breath before he was hit by the next wave and slammed down again. This was life and death in the impact zone, and there was nothing he could do except keep praying for breaths until it spit him out.

There is a strange peace and clarity that comes with helplessness. As if there is nothing else to do except wait and think. Unable to see, whether or not he opened his eyes, Kai didn't have to tell himself how stupid it had been to stay in the water after dark. With each crash of a wave and each hold down, he was reminded of the fact that he no longer had the slightest idea which direction was toward shore. He wouldn't have known where to go even if the waves had allowed him to go there.

Around and around we go, and where we stop, nobody knows . . .

Chilled, starved for oxygen, battered and bruised, Kai could feel his strength slowly draining away. Just holding his breath and trying to find the surface was exhausting. He knew he was supposed to save his energy. If he ever got out of the impact zone he'd still have to swim and fight the backwash and undertow to get to the beach. The other possibility was getting caught in a rip current and being pulled outside, where he could float and wait to regain his strength. But the water was cold and he was already freezing. In this old 3/2 wet suit he would only last so long before hypothermia rendered his arms and legs useless, his core temperature dropped, and he fell into a coma of heat loss.

What a way to go. But then, who would miss him anyway? His mom, the only person who'd ever really cared about him, was gone. He liked some of the people he'd met here in Sun Haven, but he hardly even knew them. Once he was gone, he wouldn't even be a memory.

When the hard thing banged into the side of his head, Kai assumed it was his board or a piece of driftwood. He tried to raise his arms to protect himself and was surprised at how sluggishly his freezing muscles responded. When the hard thing next hit him in the chest, he somehow managed to grab it to push it away. That's when he realized it was round and smooth. Maybe some kind of pole. And it didn't go away when he pushed at it.

So he held on.

The next thing he knew, he was being pulled.

Waves crashed on him. But somehow he

knew he had to hold on. Finally out of the impact zone, he managed to lift his head out of the water for a breath. In the moonlight he saw the dark silhouette of someone's head a few feet away. Kai realized he was holding on to a wooden oar. The person on the other end was pulling him.

A little while later his feet dragged against the sandy bottom. Kai tried to find a solid footing, but his legs folded like rubber bands, unable to support his weight. A moment after that, his knees touched the bottom. He was almost to shore now, still struggling to get his footing against the torrent of backwash rushing from the beach. Each time he lost his footing, he would slide back a little. Whoever was pulling him was struggling too.

Thirty-five

With the water less than two feet deep, Kai let go of the oar and tried to crawl on his hands and knees through the sand-choked wash toward the beach. The smaller, inside waves were still crashing on him, and each time one did, it felt like a liquid net enveloping him and trying to pull him back into the black depths. Even on his hands and knees, Kai felt himself slipping backward. If he could just stand up and get his body out of the backwash . . .

A hand clasped his arm just below his left shoulder, not pulling or pushing him, just there as if ready should he start to slip back. With his hands and knees sinking in the mushy wet sand, Kai looked up.

In the moonlight he saw Everett, seawater dripping off his drooping dreadlocks, a soaking-wet white T-shirt clinging to his body.

Too exhausted to stand, Kai crawled a short way up the beach. All he really wanted to do was collapse face first on the sand, but with Everett there he mustered every last bit of strength to sit and look back out at the dark waves. Rarely had he ever gasped so hard, or felt his heart beating so intensely. Shivers burst out of him like an earthquake, muscles all over his body jerking spasmodically, his teeth chattering uncontrollably.

Everett went to the water's edge and retrieved the oar, then came back to Kai.

"You okay?"

Kai tried to nod. His head bobbed up and down rapidly, as if he was leaning into a jackhammer. He couldn't even talk. His teeth were chattering so hard he was afraid he might bite part of his tongue off.

"You sure?" Everett asked.

Kai just shivered uncontrollably.

"I'll be right back," Everett said.

Kai couldn't imagine where the guy was going, so he didn't try. He just sat there in his wet suit, knees pulled up tight against his chest, waiting for the shivers to slow. A few moments later Everett reappeared with a bundle in his hands. "Here. Don't know if this'll help, but it probably can't hurt."

It was a damp towel, no doubt left behind by some beachgoer. Kai tried to reach out and take it, but his hands were trembling so badly he couldn't get his fingers to operate.

"Whoa, dude, let me do it." Everett draped the towel over Kai's shoulders, then sat down again. "You sure you're okay? I've never seen anyone shiver this bad."

Kai again tried to nod that he was okay. The shivers were starting to subside slightly. He and Everett sat watching the huge dark waves burst into white foam in the moonlight. Above the mist from the crashing waves, the stars came out, twinkling like distant Christmas lights.

As Kai slowly warmed up, he realized the night air had become cool now that the onshore breeze had picked up again. Next to him, Everett in his soaking-wet T-shirt and shorts was starting to shiver, though much more mildly than Kai had.

"You cold?" Kai asked.

"Not as cold as you."

"I don't know how to thank you, dude," Kai said. "For all I know you just saved my life."

"No sweat," said Everett.

"How'd you know I was out there?" Kai asked.

"Came down to the beach before. No particular reason. Sometimes I just like to watch the sunset. Saw you out there surfing. Figured I'd watch for a second. Looked like you were rippin' pretty good."

"Till I went over the falls," Kai said.

"That was a freak wave, dude. Way more than overhead. Maybe even double. We never get waves like that around here. Saw you start to take off and thought, 'What the hell is he doing? Thing's still forty feet behind him.' Then I figured out you couldn't judge it from where you were in the dark. When that thing jacked up behind you I thought, 'Man, if he catches that mother, it's gonna be the ride of his life, and if he doesn't catch it, they'll be picking up body parts for weeks to come.'"

That reminded Kai. "Seen my board?"

"Which piece?"

Kai looked up and down the water line. About twenty yards to his right, the tail of the board lay fins up on the beach. To his left the nose bobbed in the shallows.

"Guess I better put the oar back," Everett said, motioning toward the lifeguard stand. "You sure you're gonna be okay?"

Kai nodded. "Yeah. Thanks, really."

"I'll probably see Lucas later," Everett said. "Want me to tell him you won't be able to make it tomorrow morning?"

Not make it in the morning? Kai knew how that would sound. Sam telling the world, *Fricken Kai chickened out again. Guy's a total swish.*

"No way," Kai said. "You tell him I'll be here."

Everett picked up the oar and headed toward the lifeguard stand. Kai rose slowly to his feet. His legs still felt rubbery, but at least now they could support him. He reached behind and unzipped the wet suit, then peeled it down to his waist and covered his bare shoulders with the damp sandy towel and headed back to the shop.

"Where the hell you been?" Pat wanted to know when Kai showed up just before closing time.

"Had to take care of a few things," Kai said, and headed for the back.

Pat grabbed his arm. "Hold it!"

Kai stopped, and stared at Pat's hand around his bicep. "Let go."

"Or what?" his father asked.

"Or I'll make you let go."

There was an instant—almost unnoticeable if you weren't paying close attention—when Kai saw something in Pat's eyes that he'd never seen before. Just a glimmer of doubt, an uncertainty, as if he couldn't be sure Kai wouldn't rear back and slam him.

Kai felt the Alien Frog Beast's grip on his arm diminish and then disappear.

"You listen to me," Pat growled. "The only thing you have to take care of is what I tell you to take care of, understand? Otherwise you're out of here and I don't care what happens to you."

"Is that a promise?" Kai asked.

"I'm not gonna tell you again, you little punk. You can't do squat without me. You can't even prove who you are. You ain't goin' nowhere unless I say so, understand?"

Kai just gazed at him, feeling a strange mixture of anger, disgust, and pity. Pat was wrong. He could go anywhere he damn well pleased. And he would.

When the time was right.

Thirty-six

The next morning at 6 A.M., Kai opened his eyes. His shoulder was throbbing painfully and the rest of his body felt stiff and sore, as if he'd gone ten rounds in a boxing ring the previous night. Muscles he never even knew he had ached. Just sitting up on his mattress hurt, and he grimaced as he slowly got to his feet. Outside in the cool dawn air he pulled on the cold clammy wet suit. It was still damp from the previous night and it sent a chill through him, an eerie and disturbing reminder of the uncontrollable shivers he'd felt the night before. He glanced at #43. Now that the fish was broken, should he take it? No, it didn't make sense. He left it leaning against the wall behind the shop and started to walk toward the beach.

Once again he heard the lumbering thunder of the crashing waves before he saw them. When he crossed the boardwalk, this time he wasn't surprised to see the small crowd of people waiting. It still seemed strange that they cared so much about an unofficial surfing heat between a couple of local guys. Maybe there just wasn't much else going on around Sun Haven. Or maybe there was more riding on this heat than Kai realized. In the crowd were all the usual suspects, but in addition Kai was surprised to see Buzzy Frank and Dave McAllister, the manager of the boardroom at Sun Haven Surf. What did they care? Buzzy's son Lucas wasn't even surfing.

Jade was there in her hooded sweatshirt and shorts. A sleepy-looking guy with sandy hair falling into his eyes had his arm around her waist in that possessive way meant to show he was claiming her as property. Jade shoved her hands into the pockets of her sweatshirt and looked uncomfortable in the guy's grasp. She shot Kai an apologetic look, as if to say this wasn't really the way she wanted things to be. He gave her the slightest nod to show he understood.

As Kai stepped onto the beach he felt a dozen pairs of eyes on him. The sand felt cool under foot this morning, and a seagull swooped low near him to eye a plastic bag that might have contained some beak-watering leftovers. The sky was clear and the early-morning sun was yellow. In the far distance its rays glimmered off the rippled surface of the water. But closer in, there was no reflection, only green-blue perfection. The waves this morning were as close to epic macking ground swells as Sun Haven probably ever saw, smoothed and polished after a trip of a thousand miles from some tropical disturbance far to the south. Each wave peeled away with uncanny precision, the crests feathering and being blown back by the offshore breeze. Almost like blue-green horses' heads with white manes flying out behind.

Kai felt an ache. This was truly a surf-film quality morning. The perfect time to let every care and worry go and just plunge into the joy of ripping. But instead he would have to deal with the incredible BS of competition for something that should have been as free as the air.

Bean and Booger were coming up the beach toward him.

"Dude, we heard about last night," Booger said.

"The word is you got munched bad," Bean said. "That you almost died out there."

"Almost, but not quite," Kai said.

"What are you gonna do without a board?" Booger asked.

"I don't know," Kai said. "Bodysurf if I have to."

"Seriously," Bean said. "I've already asked everybody I've seen this morning, and no one's gonna lend you their stick in conditions this big. Everybody says if you don't break the board yourself, freakin' Sam'll break it for you."

"They could be right," Kai admitted.

They joined the crowd. Shauna was there and gave him a weak, hopeful smile, as if implying that she thought he was doomed, but would cheer for him anyway. Lucas and his brahs were huddled together, talking. Every now and then one of them would fire off a heavy vibe in Kai's direction. Except for Everett, who kept his eyes averted and never looked Kai's way.

Kai waited. Finally Lucas and Sam broke loose from the group and approached him.

"So what's the deal?" Sam asked. "Where's your board?"

"You know what happened to my board," Kai answered.

"Then what's the point?" Lucas asked.

"We'll decide it some other way," Kai said.

"How?" Lucas asked.

"Bashing," Kai said.

Sam turned and looked at the blue-green walls of water curling and exploding over the sandbar. He shook his head. "Piss off, dude. No fricken way am I body surfing in that. You're out of your fricken mind."

"Well, that was my answer," Kai said. "You don't like it, come up with something better."

Sam turned to Lucas. "This is bullshit. We called it a surfing heat from the beginning. You ask me, I think he showed up without a board on purpose. The tuna swish is playin' chicken shit mind games."

Kai charged. If it hadn't been for the loose sand under his feet, he would have landed a head butt square in Sam's chest, but the sand kicked out behind him like gravel under spinning tires, and by the time Kai took the next step, a pair of arms went around him from behind.

"Chill out," said Bean, locking his hands together to keep Kai from breaking loose.

Lucas stepped between Kai and Sam. "What the fuck, dude? You come here to surf or fight?"

Restrained by Bean's lassolike hold, Kai felt his hands ball into fists. He stared right at Sam. "You ever call me chicken again, I'll make a necklace out of your teeth, understand?"

Sam made a big show of smirking, but Kai could tell he was rattled.

"Look, this isn't about bashing and it isn't about fighting," Lucas said. "It's about surfing." He looked over Kai's shoulder at Bean. "Think you can control the wildman for a second?"

"I'll give it a shot, but no promises," Bean said.

Lucas walked over to where his father was standing with Dave McAllister. They started to talk. There was a lot of head shaking and shrugging on the part of Buzzy and Dave. Finally Dave nodded and started back up the beach. Lucas came back to Kai.

"We're gonna get you a board," Lucas said.

"Should be okay for today's conditions."

So they'd wait. Kai sat down on the beach with Bean, Booger, and Shauna. Lucas hung with his brahs. The rest of the small crowd milled around.

Kai noticed that some people had begun to look to their right. He followed their eyes and spied Curtis limping unsteadily down the beach, carrying a large yellow travel mug which, Kai was certain, contained the highest octane coffee/alcohol mixture allowed by law. While the others watched Curtis, Kai turned to glance at Buzzy Frank, who set his jaw and shoved his hands into his pockets. No love lost between those two, that was for sure.

Curtis stopped in front of Kai and his friends. "Waitin' for something?"

"A board," Kai said.

"I thought you made one," said Curtis.

"It met an unfortunate end."

The deep lines between Curtis's bushy eyebrows deepened more. "Then how you gonna surf against big bad Sam the sham?"

"Got anything under eight feet?" Kai asked.

Curtis glanced back toward the motel thoughtfully, then shook his head. "Sorry, grom."

Dave McAllister appeared on the board-walk carrying a red six-footer. Looked like a dual-fin swallowtail. No visible logo or markings to indicate that it was made by a manufacturer or even by an experienced shaper. Dave came down the beach and handed the board to Kai, who quickly looked it over to see how much tail and nose rocker it had. Not enough for a day like today, when Kai would have been a lot happier on a narrower pintail thruster or at least a squashtail. Something with a lot more turned up nose. But that was the whole point, wasn't it? It wasn't exactly in their interest to make it easy for him.

"You got your judges?" Lucas asked.

Kai motioned toward Bean and Booger.

"Everett and Runt will judge for us," Lucas said, holding up an air horn. "There'll be one twenty-minute heat. One blast at five minutes left. Three blasts and it's over."

Kai took the red swallowtail, strapped on the leash, and headed straight for the water.

Sam seemed to be caught off guard. "Wait a minute. Did anyone say start?"

Kai stopped and looked back at Lucas.

"Okay, guys," Lucas said. "Start."

Thirty-seven

Kai knew he was in trouble the moment he began paddling. The board pulled to the left and he suspected one of the fins was improperly placed. Not far from him Sam was thrashing through the slop, and duck diving the inside waves.

Being smaller, thinner, and presenting less resistance, Kai managed to paddle out first. A set was coming in and he knew he didn't have a second to waste. The first few rides wouldn't even be about showing what he could do. They would be purely about figuring out how to ride this messed-up board.

The wave started to crest behind him and Kai took off. Instantly, the board began to pull left. By reflex, Kai dug the heelside rail in to keep the board trimmed down the face for the speed he'd need. The board sliced sideways into the face of the wave. The nose pearled, and Kai felt himself lose it and get dusted.

He came up out of the soup in time to see Sam smack the lip and send spray high into the air. He turned and glanced at the beach. Lucas's crew was smiling. Bean and Booger stood grim faced. Someone was jogging up the beach toward the boardwalk. Kai realized that it was Shauna. He couldn't blame her for wanting to leave.

Even with a gimpy board Kai was determined to give it everything he had. If the red swallowtail wanted to go left, then he'd go left with it. On his next wave he took off straight again. This time when the board started to pull, he dug in toeside to go with it, did a sharp bottom turn, got nearly vertical on the way back up into what could have been a relatively decent move, if he hadn't charged into the falling lip and been tossed heels over head into the foam.

It was starting to become a game for Kai. Just seeing what he could get that crazy board to do was more interesting to him than competing. The board was bad only if you didn't try to use it to your advantage. In a strange way this was fun, a challenge. What sort of radical moves could Kai get a board like this to do? How much extra snap could he coax out of this thing? How freakish a cutback could it produce? Would it sideslip more easily? Could he turn a disadvantage into an advantage?

Kai wondered if that was his "problem." He just couldn't help having fun, couldn't help trying new things and taking risks instead of playing it safe and scoring "points" by executing well-practiced maneuvers. How many times could Sam smack the lip the same way, get the same fan of spray, without starting to feel bored and stale? It just didn't make sense to surf like that. You might as well have been working on the production line in a trick factory.

It wasn't that Kai had forgotten about winning. He still wanted to. But it was obvious that it wasn't going to happen in any "normal" sort of way. It was up to the board. He had to figure out what it wanted to do and help it do it.

He got so into seeing what the board

could do that he almost forgot about the time. So far Kai had tried some insane gyrations, but they'd all ended with him wiping out. If he'd been successful at any of them he might have won the whole heat on that one move alone. Meanwhile Sam never varied from his lip-smacking routine.

Kai had just wiped out again and was inside when he saw someone hurrying down the beach. It was Shauna, and at first Kai couldn't figure out what she was doing. Then another figure appeared on the boardwalk with a bright white board. With a start, Kai realized it was Teddy.

Bean and Booger started waving for him to come in. Kai paddled as hard as he could, rode in on some inside slop, jumped off the gimpy board and tried to run through the shallows and yank off his leash at the same time, which probably wasn't the smartest thing to do.

Teddy came down to the water's edge, followed by Bean, Shauna, and Booger. She presented him with the bright white board—a pintail thruster with a turned up nose. It was perfect, just what he would have asked for. Like she'd read his mind, or just knew him way better than he thought. Either way, it was totally unlike her to give him a board.

"Why are you doing this?" he asked.

"You've got nice friends," Teddy said, glancing at Shauna, who blushed.

"What if something happens to it?" Kai asked.

"You'll owe me big-time," Teddy said. "No, forget I said that. You *already* owe me big-time for this. Have fun."

"Here." Bean handed him a bar of wax. Kai put the board down and quickly drew long fat streaks up and down the deck, then strapped on the leash and headed back into the water. He was about halfway out when he heard the blast from the air horn. Five minutes to go. This was crazy. If he was incredibly lucky he might have time for one ride on a board he'd never ridden before. Had he made a mistake? Would he have been better off staying with the gimpy board and going for one last insane over-the-top maneuver?

He got back out with maybe three minutes to go. Of course, this had to be the precise moment when there'd be a lull between sets. Kai peered into the distance. There might have been a set way out there, but it was too far away to really tell. Sometimes waves that looked great from far away reared up prematurely and then settled down into useless lumps of water. Kai could practically hear the seconds ticking past in his head. There was nothing he could do. Either a wave would come or it wouldn't.

Talk about seconds stretching into minutes. It felt like the air horn should have gone off by now. Meanwhile, what he'd seen far in the distance turned out to be the set he needed. Only, would it get there before the air horn blared?

Insanely, the set came in. Kai actually wondered if the air horn had blasted and he'd somehow missed it. Maybe it didn't matter. The waves were here and he was going to take one. He saw the one he wanted and paddled into position. Teddy's bright white board cut through the water like a hot knife through butter. He took off, popped up and headed straight down the face, slashed a huge spraying bottom turn and headed back up. Suddenly he knew it was air time. He had all the momentum he needed to launch off the lip. He compressed, then sprang, swung his body around, grabbed both rails, turned one hundred and eighty degrees in the air—felt that amazing sensation of weightlessness—somehow landed it backward, twisted hard, sliding the nose around, and rode in on the soup.

Eat that for lunch, Slammin' One-Move Sam.

On the beach the small crowd hooted, clapped, and cheered. Booger and Bean were jumping around like crazy men, waving their arms and yelling. Shauna was smiling, and Teddy actually appeared to be nodding in approval.

But strangely, Lucas and his crew were exchanging high fives. Kai dropped down to the deck and started to paddle in. He didn't know what was going on. He just knew it didn't make sense.

Thirty-eight

Bean ran down the beach and splashed into the surf to give Kai a high five. "That was awesome! I mean, I don't even know what it was, but it was unreal!"

As usual, Booger was close behind Bean. "Man, I gotta tell you, that was full-on amazing. A freakin' frontside blaster. Or maybe a one-eighty or whatever. Man, I mean, like I am so relieved 'cause I gotta tell you, dude, a lot of people around here were starting to wonder if you were just a big poseur, you know? Just all talk."

Kai had to grin. "Thanks, Booger. I can always count on you to tell it like it is."

He tucked the board under his arm and

started up the beach. Teddy stood apart from the crowd. Kai walked up to her and held out the board. "Thanks."

Teddy looked down at the board and frowned. "I don't want this."

"You have to take it," Kai said. "I mean, really, I appreciate the loan, but there's no way I can keep it. I know what it costs."

Teddy shook her head. "You've got the rest of the summer to work it off."

"Are you serious?" Kai asked.

"Believe me, I'll make sure you earn it," Teddy said.

Kai couldn't help smiling. "Thanks, Teddy." He turned and headed toward Lucas. By now he had a feeling he knew what had happened.

Kai stopped in front of Lucas and his brahs. Sam had a big, turd-eating grin on his face. "Too little, too late, dude."

"Didn't you hear the air horn?" Lucas asked.

Kai shook his head. He didn't remember hearing anything. Then again, he'd been totally focused on the ride.

"Well, it went off just as you were taking off, so too bad," said Sam.

"Now why should that matter?" someone asked.

Kai turned and found Curtis coming up behind him.

"That's the way the rules work," Lucas replied.

"What rules?" Curtis asked. "A bunch of groms get together to have a surf-off and see who's better. Where's the rulebook on that?"

"We agreed it would be a twenty-minute heat," Lucas said.

"No," Curtis countered. "You said it was a twenty-minute heat. I don't believe my boy here ever agreed to it. The only thing he agreed to was to surf against your big one-trick pony."

People in the crowd sniggered. Sam turned red.

"Every surfing competition has limits," Lucas said. He glanced at Teddy, then back at Curtis. "I'm surprised you don't agree. After all, dude, you were the one who used to insist on the rules more than anyone."

Curtis appeared to grimace and his shoulders sagged under the weight of that memory. Lucas had delivered a clever and lethal shot. Still, it gave Kai the opening he'd been waiting for. "What is it with you and competing, Lucas? Is that why you surf? Just to beat everybody else? To prove you're the best? For what? A trophy? A sponsorship deal so you can make money endorsing sneakers for kids who've never even touched a surfboard? To get your picture in some surfing magazine that month after month shows the same fifty surfers on the same fifty waves? Is that all surfing means to you? Seriously, let me ask you something, brah. Have you *ever* surfed just for the pure enjoyment of it?"

The crowd went quiet. Lucas didn't seem to have an answer. He glanced at his father, as if looking for help.

"Look, here's what I think," Kai said earnestly. "There used to be one rule in surfing, but now maybe there should be two. The first is you never drop in or snake another guy's wave. The second is nobody owns a break. It's open to anyone who wants to surf. Maybe we don't have to remind each other of all the mistakes we made in the past. Maybe we don't even have to be enemies. We don't have to be friends, either, but we can share a spot and let one another surf without making this big stupid deal about it."

"That's a great idea if you don't mind getting one ride an hour," Buzzy Frank said, coming to his son's rescue. "But most of us don't have that kind of time to waste. So listen, you want to allow that last ride? Go ahead. But you have to agree that it's still up to the judges."

Thirty-nine

Bean and Booger went first. Both agreed that Kai's was the balls-out best ride of the day.

"No surprise there," Sam said with a smirk.

"What about number of rides?" Lucas asked. "What about duration and length of rides?" He turned to Runt and Everett.

"Sam won," said Runt.

"Oh, yeah?" said Bean. "I'm tempted to ask for which move? Only it doesn't matter since they were all exactly the same."

More people in the crowd chuckled. Runt narrowed his eyes and made a fist at Bean.

"Runt made his decision," Buzzy said. "Judge's decisions aren't open to debate."

Everybody turned to Everett.

Kai was curious to see what the kid would do. It was hard to imagine him going against Lucas, but after last night you never knew. And one thing Kai and everyone else did know for certain, that last ride made everything Sam had done look like kindergarten.

You could almost see Everett shrink in the glare of everyone's eyes. Kai suddenly realized the kid was in a bad position. He could side with his friends and look like a spineless wimp to everyone else. Or he could do the "right" thing, and lose his friends completely.

"Okay, forget it," Kai said. "I don't care what the decision is. It doesn't matter. Judges or no judges, everybody knows what really happened out there. I'm coming back here tomorrow, and I'm surfing Screamers. And the day after that, and the day after that, too. And so are my friends." He turned to Sam. "And no one's gonna lay a finger on them, understand?"

Kai faced Buzzy next. "You and your friends may own this town, but you don't own the waves. And you never will."

Finally, Kai looked at Lucas. "See you tomorrow. Right here."

He tucked his new board under his arm . . . and headed up the beach.

Look for the next Impact Zone book!
Cut Back
by Todd Strasser

The six surfers got outside. The air horn blew and the green flag went up. Almost immediately, pink and white tried to get rides on waves that were going nowhere. Kai had a feeling that unless one of them got incredibly lucky, those two weren't going to be much to worry about.

A set came in, and navy blue caught a wave and did a snap with a nice spray, then tried to get into the pocket again but ran out of juice. Kai knew he'd be a contender. The next wave in the set was rearing up, and both Spazzy and Kai were close enough to take it.

"Go on," Kai said.

Spazzy paddled into the wave and popped up. The wave looked like it might peel without sectioning, and rather than try a ride-ending trick, Spazzy wisely decided to go for distance and length of ride. Kai heard hoots and cheers from the beach.

Another wave was coming and Kai and the remaining surfer, a kid wearing red, paddled for it. Kai was closer to the curl so it was his ride, but the other guy either didn't see him or thought maybe he could steal the wave. With the kid blocking him and no room to go anywhere, Kai did a sharp bottom turn, went up vertical behind the other surfer and tried to get some air going over the lip. In no time his ride was over and he bailed. When his head came back out of the water, he could hear a voice distorted by a megaphone. He couldn't make out the words, but he knew the meaning: The guy in red had just been disqualified.

Since his ride had been cut short, Kai didn't have far to paddle to get outside again. By now Spazzy had come back from his long ride.

"Too bad that guy dropped in on you," Spazzy said. "Looked like a good wave."

"That's life," Kai said. "Looked like you had a good ride."

"Good? You mean great," Spazzy said. "I really lucked out."

Another set was coming in. "See if you can do it again," Kai said.

"You sure?" Spazzy asked. "I already got one."

"So get another," Kai said.

Spazzy took off on the first good wave. This one looked like it might close out ahead of him, so he threw some spray with a snap, then tried to scoot around in front of the breaking section in the hope of getting past it. The white water caught him and he bailed out.

The other guys caught some waves, but didn't do much with them. Then Kai took off on one and actually managed to get a half-decent cutback and tailslide out of it. Once again he heard hoots and cheers from the crowd on the beach.

The air horn went off again. The green flag went down and the yellow went up. As if desperate for a last chance to prove themselves, pink and white grabbed the first waves that came along and again couldn't do much with them. Spazzy caught another and smartly went for distance and duration again. Kai kept glancing at his watch, then at navy blue, and then the incoming waves. He and navy blue could almost read each other's minds. Given the choice, they both wanted the last ride. It was like a game of dare. Who'd go first? But with only five surfers in the heat and three going to the next round, Kai was already pretty certain Spazzy had made it and he had nothing to lose.

A wave came. At the last second Kai spun around. It wasn't that he was trying to fake out navy blue, but he wanted to take the wave late and the face steep, to get up enough speed to boost air. With the sound of the folding lip crackling in his ears, he took off and popped up, compressed into the bottom turn and launched off the lip, rotating as hard as he could, without a clue as to how he was going to land.

It felt sort of between a one-eighty and a flip, and the amazing thing was, he actually landed on his board before pitching headfirst into the wash. When his head popped out, it was just in time to hear the final air horn and see the yellow flag come down and the red one come up.

The first heat was over.

Todd Strasser is the author of more than one hundred novels for teens and middle graders including the best-selling Help! I'm Trapped In . . . series. His novels for older teens include *The Accident, The Wave, Give a Boy a Gun,* and *Can't Get There from Here.* Todd and his kids have surfed Hawaii, California, and the eastern seaboard from Florida to New York.

Check Your PULSE Book Club

Sign up for the CHECK YOUR PULSE
free teen e-mail book club!

 **FEATURING**

A new book discussion every month

Monthly book giveaways

Chapter excerpts

Book discussions with the authors

Literary horoscopes

Plus YOUR comments!

To sign up go to www.simonsays.com/simonpulse and
don't forget to CHECK YOUR PULSE!

As many as 1 in 3 Americans
who have HIV... don't know it.

TAKE CONTROL.
KNOW YOUR STATUS.
GET TESTED.

To learn more about HIV testing,
or get a free guide to HIV and
other sexually transmitted diseases:

www.knowhivaids.org
1-866-344-KNOW